# Postmaster General

*Every street has its secrets*

By Spencer D Hawkes

Dedicated to 'Mummy'. For all that you do and all that you have done.

**Street Press**
London

Copyright © 2025 by Spencer D. Hawkes

The moral right of the author is hereby asserted in accordance with The Copyright, Designs and Patents Act 1988.

All characters and events in this publication, other than those clearly in the public domain, are fictitious and any resemblance to actual persons, living or dead, is purely coincidental.

All rights reserved. No part of this publication may be reproduced, stored in a retrieval system, or transmitted, in any form or by any means without the prior written permission of the publisher, nor be otherwise circulated in any form of binding or cover other than that in which it is published and without a similar condition being imposed on the subsequent buyer.

A CIP catalogue record for this book is available from the British Library.

ISBN 9798284387979
Typeset by Abdul Rehman
Cover design by Street Press

# Foreword

Some people live quiet lives.
Some people live dangerous ones.
Ian Taylor lives both.

On paper – and there is a lot of paper – Ian is a mid-level marketing manager at the Post Office. He's the kind of man whose lunches come in clingfilm, whose socks never quite match, and who once confused an oat milk latte with industrial cleaner (and yet drank it anyway).

He has a large, mostly obedient dog named Tolstoy, a wife who has mastered the art of disappointed silence, and a deep commitment to eating crisps in situations where crisps should not be eaten. His children are smart, well-educated, and slightly baffled by the man who raised them while smelling faintly of gravy and surgical spirit.

He forgets birthdays. He forgets bin day. He forgets to shower.

But he never forgets to check the locks. Or scan a room. Or listen when no one's speaking.

Behind the flecks of gravy on his jumper, behind the lingering smell of bin juice, lies something else entirely:

This is a tale about a man who seems harmless... until you look a little closer.

Welcome to his world.
The tea's on.
The dog's armed.
Proceed with caution.

**~ Spencer D. Hawkes**

# Contents

*Chapter 1*
**Signed, Sealed, Executed** 11

*Chapter 2*
**Crumbs and Codes** 35

*Chapter 3*
**No Smoke Without Fire** 53

*Chapter 4*
**Daddy Issues** 71

*Chapter 5*
**The Toast of Tehran** 85

*Chapter 6*
**A Clean Break** 109

*Chapter 7*
**A Man of Taste** 133

*Chapter 8*
**A Broken Spaniel** 149

Chapter One
# Signed, Sealed, Executed

*"We make tidy places to keep untidy things from showing."*
**~ Sir John Betjeman (possibly)**

# Chapter 1

# Signed, Sealed, Executed

There was a certain grim poetry to Ian Taylor's mornings, if you squinted hard enough. Out in the leafy sprawl of North London – where people pay obscene money to live near identikit coffee shops and pretend where they live is still a village – Ian Taylor's house sat quietly on a suburban street lined with respectable, finely clipped hedges and double-glazed dreams.

A place where life marched on in orderly bins and weary sighs.

The street was a polite battle of appearances: fresh gravel driveways, tasteful olive trees in terracotta pots, and boxy hatchbacks that were somehow always just clean enough. Gardens fought for dominance with hanging baskets and perfectly tormented rose bushes. Small, desperate status symbols for people who still argued passionately about recycling and hedge heights.

Ian's house fitted in – almost.

His was a slightly sagging detached house with flaking paint on the windowsills and an aging cat-flap that had never even seen a cat. Well, certainly not while Ian and his family had lived there, which was about 19 years – give or take a month or two.

But something about it still charmed in its own shabby chic way.

Wisteria twisted up around the brickwork in languid sweeps, its purple flowers spilling over the porch in spring like an aristocrat's hair gone feral. Honeysuckle knotted through the trellis, determined and unbothered by pruning attempts, filling the air with a heavy, sweet scent that clung long after the sun had dipped each day.

Framing the front door, the plants looked almost too romantic for the building they belonged to – like someone had tried to woo a bus shelter with poetry.

And then there was the door itself: heavy oak, proudly original, a relic from the Arts and Crafts era. The centrepiece of which was a stained-glass window, featuring a once bold, beautiful image of a coloured glass tulip rising from a bed of stylised leaves. Now it was cracked in two places, one petal held together with an ancient smear of discoloured superglue and a more recent strip of Sellotape, as a backup measure, giving the angular glass flower a faintly apologetic tilt. When the sun caught it just right – around five-thirty on a good evening – the hallway would flood with fractured light, scattering red and green and gold across the battered laminate flooring like a broken promise. Most of the time, though, the door just creaked ominously and let in the smell of next door's overcooked cabbage.

Inside, the house was a shifting, gentle wreck: furniture chosen for comfort and practicality rather than style, carpets that had seen better decades, a kitchen clinging stubbornly to its late '90s aesthetic. Not a sniff of modern flatpack furniture here.

And yet, there was warmth in the chaos – the kind of muddled, scruffy comfort that came from years of living, not staging.

It wasn't perfect.

It wasn't even close.

But it was home.

And for Ian Taylor – a man built out of stubbornness, stains, and questionable breakfasts – that was more than enough.

Ian Taylor had the look of a man who had been assembled in a hurry and left out in the rain. Tall, broad, not so much built as cobbled together, he carried the kind of heft that could have been muscle once, but now slumped into thick, heavy lines. His clothes were an afterthought: jeans frayed at the cuffs, shirts stained with the slow, quiet disasters of his daily life. Gravy flecks, porridge splashes and suspiciously large crumbs of various foods that clung to him and his beard like barnacles.

Hygiene had always been more theory than practice for Ian. At school, he'd been the kid nobody wanted to sit next to – the one with the odd smell and a worrying fascination with picking at his own nose. Decades later, not much had changed. His socks were a tragedy, his shoes crushed flat from years of lazy shuffling, and his general atmosphere suggested someone who had fought a valiant but losing battle against soap and lost the will to try again. He didn't just look very ordinary – he looked like the reason most people moved a seat away on public transport.

Inside of number 43 Pembroke Avenue, Ian's house, chaos reigned.

In the kitchen, one of those once smart, granite-surfaced affairs dreamed up by catalogues and desperation, Ian stood at the now chipped and worn hob, waging war against a poor defenceless saucepan.

He was stirring something that might once have been porridge, if you were feeling generous. Now it was a lumpy, steaming mass, somewhere between wallpaper paste and a chemical accident.

Susan, Ian's long-suffering wife, watched him from across the room, arms folded, dressing gown sagging at the shoulders. Her face carried the patient resentment of a woman who'd long ago abandoned the fantasy of being married to someone competent.

Yet it was clear they both loved one another very much, and they still continuously called one another 'Mummy' and 'Daddy'. This was a hangover from when their two children were still very young, and they had never quite dropped the habit. It continued now, even though Daisy and Max were both grown up and desperate to escape this Kafkaesque suburban hellhole for a place of their own. They were both just waiting for mortgage rates to drop, or the cost of houses to go down – or ideally both. It was either that or they would have to live in Watford, or worse still, Welwyn Garden City.

"That's not porridge," Susan said to Ian, in the tone of someone identifying a crime scene. "That's soup with identity issues."

Ian, undeterred, flashed a grin. His teeth were a patchy battleground between yellow and defiance.

"Morning Mummy. It's porridge-related," he said to his Wife proudly.

Susan exhaled slowly through her nose.

"For God's sake, Daddy, just let me do it." She elbowed him aside, snatching the spoon from his hand with the finality of someone removing a loaded gun from a troublesome toddler.

Ian shuffled away, muttering.

"It's Nouvelle Cuisine porridge. Modern culinary expression!"

"It's an expression of how bleeding useless you are," she said, banging another saucepan onto the hob. "And have you put that bloody bin out yet?"

Ian wobbled slightly, as if the question had physically struck him. "I'm pacing myself. Building up to it."

"Listening ears, Daddy. Listening ears. I asked you to do it twice last night." She jabbed the air with a spoon. "It's still there. Like those bloody smelly socks of yours sitting in the middle of the hall all week!"

"I'm letting them air," Ian said defensively, as if this were a valid lifestyle choice.

Then he burped – a low, vibrating sound like a tuba played underwater – and shuffled out of the kitchen, trailing the faint aroma of stale crisps, whisky and regret behind him.

In the hallway, he stepped carefully over Tolstoy – a hulking mass of black fur and baleful eyes – the Russian Black Terrier who treated the rest of the family like mildly interesting intruders but adored Ian with terrifying loyalty.

"Morning, Tolstoy," Ian said, reaching down to scratch the big dog's belly.

Tolstoy growled – a sound more warning than welcome – and then, begrudgingly, rolled over for Ian, presenting an enormous patch of fur that could easily conceal a large weapon or two.

From the living room, Max's voice drifted out.

"Why does the dog only respect you? He terrifies everyone else."

Ian smirked. "Maybe he knows something you all don't." It wasn't a boast. It was simply a truth nobody here seemed particularly interested in uncovering.

At 26 years of age, Max Taylor had the look of someone who'd just stepped out of a minimalist lifestyle blog – all clean lines, good lighting, and an inexplicable number of moisturisers. Fair hair that always seemed effortlessly ruffled in just the right way. Slim build. Clear skin. Good posture, like someone who'd never had to eat cold Findus Crispy Pancakes, with baked beans, over a sink – because he didn't possess a plate.

He dressed with quiet intent – Oxford shirts worn open at the neck, sleeves rolled precisely two turns, expensive trainers in colours that didn't exist ten years ago. Casual, yes, but curated. The sort of casual that said: "I work in finance, but I still care about oat milk and mental health."

He was a trader for a towering Swiss bank in the City, where he translated vast amounts of money into spreadsheets, risk reports, and vague words like 'structural margin volatility.' Nobody in the family understood what he actually did, but it came with a gym membership, and he seemed happy enough.

Max had a soft spot for his mum, tolerated his sister, and – oddly – seemed to actually quite like his dad. Or at least, he didn't write Ian off quite as quickly as the two women in the household seemed to do. Where Daisy saw a disaster, Max occasionally saw... well, something else.

He'd never say it. But sometimes he watched Ian the way a cat watches a laser pointer. Not pouncing. Just tracking. Trying to figure out where it would land next.

\*\*\*

In the kitchen, Ian's Daughter Daisy, an avocado-toast, quinoa munching 28-year-old, green-biro-wielding, professional disappointment detector – barely glanced up from her phone as Ian shuffled back in.

"You stink of bin juice, Tosser," she said cheerfully.

Ian beamed. "Thank you, my flower." He noticed her scribbling notes on a crumpled pad of paper in green ink. "You know," he said, with the solemnity of a man imparting state secrets, "Hitler always wrote in green."

"And you've got a bogey on your jumper, so don't start on me," Daisy replied, not looking up.

Ian glanced down. A hard green lump of crud clung defiantly to the fabric, somewhere south of his left nipple. "Adds character," he declared. "It's my brand logo." He farted loudly, as if to punctuate the moment. Daisy wrinkled her nose in theatrical disgust. "Tragic man."

"Maybe I'm really a MI5 operative," Ian said defensively, adopting a mock-serious tone. "Hidden in plain sight."

"If you were," Daisy muttered, "we'd all be dead. You can't even work the bleedin' toaster Dad."

No one laughed.

No one even paused.

In this house, the idea of Ian Taylor doing anything remotely competent – never mind being something like a spy – was absurd enough to be dismissed without thought.

It suited him just fine.

Daisy Taylor looked like someone who'd accidentally walked into the wrong family on her way to a modelling contract. Tall, blonde, yoga-limbed and permanently sun-kissed, she gave off the cool, effortless confidence of someone who'd never had to use public transport in the rain or eat crisps for dinner.

She worked in cryptocurrency, which meant she was sporadically vaguely rich, slightly cryptic, and often dialled into meetings from places that didn't have pavements. Her last six months had been conducted from a surf shack in Costa Rica, where she juggled blockchain strategy with daily dawn patrols, drank smoothies made of fruits Ian couldn't pronounce, and occasionally appeared on Zoom calls with sea spray in her fringe and parrots screaming in the background.

She was very bright – frighteningly so – and had once explained the mechanics of decentralised finance to Susan using three satsumas and a spoon. Nobody in the family had understood a word of it, but Daisy had made her point: she was from another world. What's more, she was consistently dismissive of Ian.

To her, he was a living warning against aging badly – all bad posture, weird smells, and the constant ambient threat of a burp. She called him 'Tosser' more often than 'Dad' and treated his domestic presence like he was a fault in the house's plumbing.

Still, she had a sharp sense of humour, a moral compass (albeit solar-powered and slightly misaligned), and a fondness for Tolstoy, who tolerated her only slightly more than Ian tolerated her.

Despite everything, there were moments – rare, blink-and-you'll-miss-them – when Daisy watched her father just a second too long. As if something didn't quite add up.

***

Outside, London sulked under a grey sky, clouds heavy enough to suggest rain but too indecisive to commit.

Ian braced himself for his (almost) daily pilgrimage to work at Post Office headquarters, where he worked as a middle level marketing man – who handled all the boring customer communications that nobody else wanted to do. It was dangerous work, but someone had to do it, he mused as he prepared to leave the house.

The front door groaned on its hinges as he heaved it open.

Leafy suburbia sprawled ahead: identical houses with prim front gardens, all pretending to be a little more middle-class than they really were. Bins stood lined up straight, like obedient soldiers, and somewhere a small child was crying about a spilt designer yogurt.

Ian closed the door behind him with a clatter, shouldered a battered rucksack holding his laptop, and set off down the street a lumbering, shambolic figure in a stained jacket, brandishing a half-eaten bag of crisps in one hand and a plastic bottle of brandy in the other. Food of champions he told himself – full of minerals and vitamins, all the main food groups. Commuters marched past him with grim efficiency – as he stumbled along – smart suits, briefcases, desperate lattes clutched like life preservers.

They barely noticed him.

He was part of the furniture of the street.

A grubby old sofa nobody admitted owning.

Near a bus stop, he dropped the empty crisp packet into a bin with exaggerated precision, missing twice before managing to do it on the third attempt.

A woman in Lycra jogged past, wrinkling her nose at the aura of salt, grease, and second-hand brandy that lingered around Ian.

He smiled serenely after her. She didn't know how lucky she was.

Ian arrived at the station just as the 08:14 exhaled onto the platform in a hiss of brakes and stale air.

The station itself was a relic of a bygone era, crumbling Victorian red-brick wrapped in a cage of 1980s scaffolding and pigeon netting, half-heartedly preserved by a local historical society no one remembered joining. Paint flaked from wrought-iron columns. The old station clock was stuck permanently at 12:41. Moss crept along the edges of the roof tiles like mould on an old sandwich.

Pigeons ruled here. Big, stupid ones with missing toes and eyes that blinked sideways. They strutted between commuters like they owned the place, occasionally launching into low, lazy flutters of indignation whenever someone got too close.

Ian trudged across the slick, gum-spattered platform with the weary gait of a man who'd seen too many Mondays. He wiped a streak of unidentified grime from his coat sleeve and joined the heaving knot of bodies near the yellow line, just as the train wheezed to a halt. The doors opened with the enthusiasm of a man attending his third divorce hearing – slow, squealing, and reluctant. A wave of sour commuter heat spilled out, thick with damp coats, overpriced spilt coffee, and the defeated silence of middle-class suffering.

Nobody got off.

The crowd surged forward anyway.

Ian braced and dived into the melee.

He wedged himself inside just before the doors shuddered closed behind him, his bag squashed against a stranger's shin and his right foot half-consuming the hem of a woman's expensive-looking skirt.

He found himself elbowed between a teenager blasting rap music through leaky headphones, head bobbing slightly, and an elderly man gripping a copy of *Practical Beekeeping* with the kind of intensity usually reserved for the latest porn magazine back when people bought such things. The man read at a 45-degree angle, eyes darting over the page like he was about to explode.

The train lurched into motion. Ian swayed, caught himself on a metal pole that had been polished to a soft, greasy sheen by a thousand reluctant sweaty hands. He inhaled deeply. And then regretted it.

Around him: the usual menagerie.

A woman in running gear who very much hadn't run.

A man in a pinstripe suit with halitosis strong enough to kill houseplants.

A screaming baby, somewhere, just beginning to realise it hated being alive.

The Tannoy crackled half-heartedly about a signal failure outside Kings Cross, but no one listened. It was background noise now – part of the symphony of wheezing brakes, polite coughs, muffled rage.

Ian exhaled.

Another day.

Another journey into the world of respectable tedium.

Ian emerged out into the smoggy sunlight at St Pancras Station and started his daily forced march along the Pentonville Road, blinking like a mole. He started his 20-minute hike towards the Post Office Headquarters building, evading tramps, drug dealers and cyclists in tight Lycra as he walked.

He adjusted his jacket, wiped crisp crumbs from his chest with one grubby sleeve, and sauntered toward the monolithic building where he worked.

A combination of 1950s corporate pride, new modern glass and steel loomed above him, the Post Office's headquarters – a gleaming monument to corporate bureaucracy and process. The irony was not lost on Ian.

Before stepping inside the building, he dropped the now empty brandy bottle into a recycling bin outside with a clunk, then checked his reflection in the glass: hair greasy and uncooperative, shirt rumpled, a suspicious stain blooming near his right hip.

Perfect. He was ready for his day of mediocrity and tedium.

He walked into the reception area with a toothy smile. He was amongst friends here. The security guards waved him through without even bothering to check his pass. They loved him. Mostly because he acknowledged and praised them regularly.

Ian Taylor: known entity. Local legend. A dishevelled relic of Statutory Communications.

"Morning, Ian!" called out one of the receptionists, a young, pretty woman with cartoonishly perfect teeth and stylish hair extensions.

"Morning, sunshine," Ian replied, giving her a finger-gun and an exaggerated wink. He hit the lift button with the heel of his hand and waited, humming tunelessly under his breath.

The lift doors pinged open, and Ian shuffled in.

He climbed out onto the First Floor to see who was about.

The office was already half-lit, the hum of strip lights flickering overhead like an anxious thought. The air smelled faintly of toner and boredom.

Alison, one of Ian's co-workers, was already at her desk – blonde, pretty, petite, smiling. She was one of the few people in the office who actually seemed to like Ian. In fact, she seemed to hero worship him! She listened when he spoke. She laughed – unironically – at his jokes. It was a bit unnerving for Ian. He wasn't used to it.

Her fringe was cut with surgical precision. Her blouse – pale blue with little swallow motifs – was immaculately pressed, and her heels clicked with the quiet determination of a woman who had done a power walk all the way to work at 6.30am.

She was thumbing frantically at her phone with the kind of concentrated panic usually reserved for surgeons or social media managers during a PR crisis.

She'd joined a year ago from Sky Media, where she'd apparently been a media assistant – though what that entailed no one was entirely sure. Ian suspected it mostly involved ordering pastries for meetings and nodding enthusiastically during long PowerPoint presentations. Still, she'd taken to her new role in the Post Office marketing department with baffling cheer – absorbing acronyms and procedures like a sponge dipped in single cream. "Morning, Alison," Ian said, nudging her gently with his elbow in what he intended as a casual greeting. Unfortunately, it came off somewhere between a nudge and a barge. "Oh!" she jumped, startled, clutching her phone like it had just confessed to something scandalous. Then she looked up and smiled – bright, warm, utterly disarming.

"I'm so glad you're in," she said breathlessly, as if he were oxygen. "Can I ask you something later?"

Ian blinked. He wasn't used to this level of eagerness unless it involved someone needing help changing the toner in a photocopier.

"Of course," he said, straightening his tie in the vague hope it might distract from the gravy fleck near his collar. "I'll be up on the Second floor, if I can find a desk."

Alison beamed, then turned back to her screen, fingers already flying across her keyboard in the kind of rapid, purposeful flurry that suggested either extreme competence or trying to look busy.

*What on earth did she see in him,* he asked himself? *Still... it was nice to be liked.*

Ian jumped back into the open lift. He didn't want to sit with anyone he knew, or he would be forced to talk to them all day and he had other plans. The lift jolted upward. Ian coughed wetly into his sleeve.

The Second floor was pretty much like the First floor. Both were grey on grey. Grey carpets, grey walls, grey faces. The interior design screamed aspiration meets despair. Rows of cubicles stretched into the middle distance like tiny bureaucratic cells. Each one home to a defeated soul hunched over spreadsheets, coffee cups, and the quiet hum of dying dreams.

Ian slumped into a chair, a battered relic of office furniture that groaned with familiarity under his weight.

He pulled out another bag of crisps and a can of Coke, breakfast number three, and began eating with slow, methodical crunches.

"A man's soul lives in his keyboard," he muttered, brushing and blowing crumbs off the battered plastic keys.

His inbox blinked aggressively at him:

*Customer Mailing Deadlines*

*Welsh translation rules and regulations*
*Compliance Reminder: GDPR Awareness Quiz*
*Mandatory Fire Warden Training*
Ian laughed and opened none of them.

He was considering the tactical implications of faking a fire alarm when Alison arrived by his desk, looking earnest, notebook in hand.

"When we mail letters to customers," she asked, leaning in, "does it have to be within 28 days of generating the original data extract?"

Ian chewed thoughtfully. "Yes. Spot on," he said finally, spraying a small mist of crisp crumbs onto his keyboard. "If the data extract was made longer ago than 28 days, it will need a refresh and we'll need to rerun the data – or it won't comply with GDPR best practice."

"I knew that you'd know," Alison said, smiling

*Was that a flirt,* he wondered? *Or just pity?*

"You're like a Data Ninja," she continued

"I do the dull stuff," Ian said modestly. "Regulatory comms, Tariff, Terms & Conditions. It's really not all that exciting."

"I bet you could teach me a thing or two," Alison said, lightly touching his hand, making Ian jump, sending his mouse skittering across the desk's smooth surface.

Ian, startled, took a gulp of Coke and immediately began choking.

His coughing fit was still in full swing when Ruth – mid-thirties, rat like, dark haired, ambitious, corporate power-blazer, soul eaten alive by senior management – swooped down on Ian.

"Well, well, well," she said with a thin smile. "Nice of you to grace us with your presence, Ian."

He grinned up at her through watery eyes. "Just checking you're coping OK, boss."

"You should come in more often," Ruth said, arms folded. "HR's on at me again about you – they don't like all this remote working. Might be nice to take a bath too?"

Ian widened his eyes innocently. "Thought you'd never ask."

Ruth's nostrils flared. "On your own I meant", she exclaimed irritably. She stalked away, her high stiletto heels stabbing the carpet with surgical precision.

Ian leaned back in his chair and sighed. The glamorous life he thought.

"Buzz. Buzz"

His other phone – a sleek black encrypted device nobody else at Post Office knew about – vibrated violently in his pocket. He fished it out carefully, shielding the screen from prying eyes. The message on the encrypted display blinked coldly:

*ENCRYPTED LINE 7 – PRIORITY ZULU*

He didn't react outwardly. Just stretched, yawned theatrically, and wandered off toward the toilets. He quickly dived into a vacant cubicle, locked the door behind him and perched on the edge of the closed toilet seat.

He pressed a button on the phone.

A voice, modulated and cold, filled the tiny space.

*Asset Two-Nine. ALERT! Threat may be close to your home. Possible fox in the coop. Potential perimeter breach. Be ready. Keep your eyes open.*

"Click". Line dead.

Ian flushed automatically, more out of habit than need, and shuffled back toward his desk.

Nothing to see here. Just another Monday.

The day continued in a typically tedious and deeply boring way, which mostly involved Ian arranging to get large numbers of letters printed and mailed out to customers, telling them postal prices were about to go up again and services were being reduced.

Later that evening when he got back home, Ian sat on the sagging sofa, one hand buried in yet another family-sized bag of crisps, the other idly flipping channels on the flat screen TV on the wall.

Susan sat nearby, leafing through a gardening catalogue with the faint air of someone wondering how she'd ended up here.

Ian got up and started towards the kitchen.

"If you're making tea," she said without looking up, "use the kettle. Not that microwave mug thing. And make me one too"

Ian grunted in acknowledgement. "OK Mummy,"

In the kitchen, he filled the kettle under the tap.

Something metallic clinked somewhere deep in the garden.

"Cats, probably," he muttered. "Bloody cats. Or a fox".

In truth, Ian suspected this might be the 'Fox' that his handler had warned him about earlier, via his encrypted phone earlier. He decided to investigate. He took the kettle of boiling water with him as he stepped quietly into the back garden to take a closer look. Tolstoy followed, muscles rippling under his thick black fur, a silent dark shadow of menace.

The shed at the bottom of the garden was unremarkable from the outside: peeling paint, a rusted padlock, the faint scent of damp wood.

Inside, it told a very different story.

Ian locked the shed door behind him, reached behind a sagging shelf loaded with small terracotta pots, and pressed a hidden switch. A panel slid aside with a soft, smooth hiss. Behind it: an arsenal.

High-tech rifles, semi-automatic pistols, silencers, a grenade or two, even a small broadside mine, body bags, encrypted comms equipment, and a slightly faded Union Jack.

Tolstoy sat at attention; ears pricked. Ian glanced down at him.

"Reporting for duty, eh boy?"

The dog thumped his tail once in reply.

Ian selected a semi-automatic pistol, professionally screwing on its silencer, then tucked it into his waistband, slipped military grade night-vision goggles around his neck, and pulled a heavy-duty body bag from a hook. Tonight was not a night for subtlety.

The back garden was inky pitch black, almost impossible to see, well unless you had a pair of state-of-the-art night-vision goggles.

Ian slipped out of the shed like a shadow given shape. His heavy pistol nestled against the small of his back, reassuring and familiar.

The garden stretched out before him: a postage stamp of soggy grass and stubborn weeds, the borders choked with dying herbs Susan kept insisting she'd "revive this year." The moon was a thin smear overhead.

This didn't matter of course; he had his goggles on and anyway Ian's feet knew this ground the way a drinker knows the way home from the pub – unsteady but certain.

Somewhere near the back hedge, a dark figure shifted.

Too tall for an actual fox.

Too clumsy for a cat.

Ian crouched low behind the battered compost bin, heart beating a calm, slow, steady rhythm.

The figure was fiddling with something metallic – wire cutters by the look of it. He was cutting through the rear fence.

*Amateur hour*, thought Ian.

He raised the kettle full of boiling water, still steaming, and moved fast, a surprising blur for a man of his stature.

The figure barely had time to register movement before the water splashed across his face, hands and forearms.

The muffled scream was cut short by the quiet pop of Ian's suppressed semi-automatic pistol. A single shot.

The man's body crumpled through the cut fence and into the herb bed, flattening Susan's prized mint plants.

Ian exhaled slowly and calmly through his nose. Target neutralized. No fuss, not much noise. Just another small tragedy in the dark.

He knelt, fingers moving with grim efficiency. He was like a completely different man, quick, efficient, good at what he was doing.

Body bag unfurled. Bullet casing picked up and carefully pocketed. Pistol wiped clean and holstered. Night-vision goggles back around his neck.

Tolstoy padded forward, sniffed the corpse once, and then, finding it unsatisfactory, flopped down beside Ian to chew thoughtfully on a stick.

"Stay," Ian said under his breath.

The dog thumped his tail once again in clear acknowledgment of his orders.

Minutes later, the body was zipped up in the bag, the garden returned to a vague approximation of normality, and Ian was slipping back toward the house whistling to himself – empty kettle swinging casually from his fingers.

He arrived surprisingly calmly back in the kitchen a few moments later.

Susan hadn't moved. She was still in the living room, half-watching a nature documentary, half-reading about low-maintenance perennials.

Ian refilled the kettle, set it back on its base and flicked it on, the blue LED glowing innocently.

"Think it was a fox, Mummy," he called out to Susan.

"Oh?" came her distracted reply.

"Gone now. Doubt it'll be back."

Susan appeared at the kitchen doorway, peering out suspiciously toward the garden. "Did it shit in my herb bed again?"

"Don't think so," Ian said, pouring the boiling water into two chipped, bright red mugs. "Anyway, I think I've put the wind up it. Don't think it will pester us again."

Susan grunted, satisfied.

Ian dropped a teabag into the two Post Office branded mugs and stirred slowly, staring out the window at where the body had fallen.

Herbs could be replanted.

Lives couldn't.

Several hours later the house dozed peacefully, everyone breathing in quiet, uneven patterns. Well, apart from Ian.

Susan curled up on her side, book long abandoned on the nightstand.

Ian lay flat on his back, hands folded on his chest, staring at the ceiling mulling things over.

Tolstoy lay curled at the foot of the bed, one ear twitching every few minutes.

"It's lovely, isn't it?" Susan mumbled, waking momentarily, without opening her eyes. "When you know someone so well. Like we do. No surprises. Just comfort."

Ian turned his head slightly to look at her. "I agree," he said softly.

She reached out blindly, half asleep, clumsily stroking his arm.

He held her hand.

"Love you, Daddy."

"Love you too, Mummy," Ian replied.

The room settled back into silence.

The only light came from the blinking LED light of Ian's special encrypted phone, charging quietly, hidden under the bed.

***

Later that night, once Ian was certain that everyone was completely asleep, he climbed back out of bed to go and 'tidy up a bit'.

In the garden, the shed door swung open once more.

Ian heaved the heavy body bag down through a narrow trapdoor beneath the shed floorboards. Disposal would need to be arranged. Ian would have to organise this.

Back inside the hidden compartment in the shed, he tapped out a message on his encrypted phone.

*FOX DEALT WITH. BUT WILL NEED CLEANER. USUAL PLACE.*

Seconds later, a reply buzzed in:

*NO PROBLEM. WILL ARRANGE CLEANER. MEET AT LAUNDERETTE, 12 NOON TOMORROW. HAVE A NEW PROJECT FOR YOU. WE'LL ALSO NEED YOU TO KEEP A CLOSE EYE ON THIS PERSON OF INTEREST – LIVING IN YOUR AREA.*

There was an attachment. Ian wiped his mouth absently with the back of his hand and opened the attached file. A photo flickered into view:

A smiling, balding man, watering roses in a perfectly manicured garden. Ian recognised him instantly. It was Ian's neighbour who lived just three doors down the road from his house.

Underneath: *DUFFY, MALCOLM – NEIGHBOUR – STATUS: OBSERVE.*

Ian snorted under his breath. "Those bloody perfect roses were a dead giveaway." "I knew he was a wrong 'un! Nobody ever has such perfect roses. Not unless it's a cover story," he muttered to himself cynically.

He closed the file and shut off the phone.

Tomorrow was already shaping up to be a busy day.

*\*\**

The next morning Ian was up early. He had walked Tolstoy at 6am, trying not to look too conspicuous as he leered over Mr Duffy's garden fence to see if he could spot any suspicious activity. All was quiet, so Ian decided to go home to see what he could see from one of his bedrooms.

Sunlight slashed through the morning mist, catching on the shiny bonnets of Range Rovers and modest BMWs.

Ian watched Mr. Duffy through a gap in the curtains of the spare bedroom, cradling a piping hot mug of strong tea, Tolstoy pressed against his leg.

Mr. Duffy – rotund, cheerful-looking, watering can in hand – was now out fussing over his rose bushes with tender devotion.

The dog gave a low, questioning rumble.

"Not yet, boy," Ian murmured. "Let him bloom a bit first." The suburban street outside hummed into life: Kids dragged heavy backpacks toward school. A woman walked down the pavement, not looking where she was going, cursing into her mobile. A man jogging past the house with the broken gait of someone who hated every second of it. Life carried on. And Ian Taylor – flatulent, shambolic, grubby, invisible – smiled faintly to himself. Hidden in plain sight. Just the way he liked it.

Chapter Two
# Crumbs and Codes

*"Appear harmless. Act forgettable. Kill cleanly."*
**~ MI5 Basic Fieldcraft Guide for new recruits**

## Chapter 2

# Crumbs and Codes

There are crimes, and then there are abominations. Ian Taylor's breakfast this morning fell firmly into the second category.

The kitchen table groaned under the weight of his culinary sins. A croissant, sliced lengthways with brutal disregard for tradition, sagged under a slick of butter thicker than an investment banker's bonus. Raspberry jam oozed from both halves, dripping lazily onto his already stained tie – a grim tapestry of mustard, coffee, and whatever the hell that green smudge was.

Ian smacked his lips happily and took another enormous bite of oozing croissant.

"Bloody delicious," he muttered around a mouthful of pastry and pride – spitting fragments of croissant everywhere.

Daisy wandered in, phone in hand, pausing mid-scroll. The look on her face suggested she'd stumbled upon a ritual sacrifice.

"Dad," she said, voice brittle. "Croissants are already made from butter you know. They don't need any more butter spreading on them."

Ian beamed at her, thick jam glistening on his chin. "Which makes them ideal for *extra* butter," he proclaimed loudly.

Daisy gagged theatrically. "I'm going to vomit. It looks like a crime scene."

Susan breezed in next, robe tied tight around her waist, hair scraped back into a no-nonsense bun. Her eyes narrowed at the table.

"Daddy," she said in that tone – the one that usually preceded carpet shampooing. "What on earth are you doing to those croissants?"

"Hello Mummy," Ian said, saluting with his jam-laden breakfast. "I'm assassinating them. A murder most foul of a poor, defenceless pastry."

Daisy slumped into a chair, groaning. "And why do you two cretins still call each other 'Mummy' and 'Daddy'?" she said. "You sound like pervy dolls."

"It's a symbol," Ian said loftily. "Of our deep and eternal love, for each other and for you two kids."

"And the fact I birthed a large screaming watermelon. Twice," Susan added dryly, fishing a glob of jam off the table with a wet wipe.

"Watermelons now with University degrees," Ian pointed out proudly.

Tolstoy, lurking under the table like a hungry bear, caught a blob of jam midair with the ease of a professional goalkeeper.

Ian grinned. "He understands."

"He's the only one who does," Daisy muttered, returning to her phone.

Outside, the morning sunlight limped across the street. Another glorious day in leafy north London had begun.

Ian caught the underground to Kings Cross and thought about Mr Duffy as he travelled. Once out at Kings Cross, he trudged along the pavement to work with the air of a man deeply wronged by the universe. By the time Ian reached his office, his tie was somehow even dirtier than when he had left home.

A crisp packet flapped in his hand. He took a final swig from his battered hip flask – the holy sacrament of bad habits – before slipping it back into his jacket pocket before entering Post Office HQ.

A fat pigeon watched him disapprovingly from a lamppost.

Ian ignored it. He had bigger fish to fry.

As always, the security guards in the Post Office HQ reception barely glanced up as he slouched past. He was part of the furniture here – a battered old armchair nobody could be bothered to replace. A national treasure of sorts.

The receptionist gave him a polite nod. He nodded back, suppressing a belch. Business as usual. Another day another Dollar.

Ian made a beeline for his work locker, which creaked open with the reluctant sigh of something abused for too long. Inside, amongst the layers of paper, leaflets, crushed crisp packets. a Post-It note stuck to the door with 'Sort It Out, Ian' written in Ruth's handwriting, and, half-buried under a broken stapler, sat a smart, expensive looking keyring with several high security keys. Ian pocketed it with casual precision.

"Just a quick pop-in," he murmured, more to himself than to anyone else.

No one answered. They never did.

Ian then set himself up at a desk well away from anyone who knew who he was. He didn't have time for pointless chitter chatter. The cubicle farm stretched out like a monument to lost hope – an endless graveyard of lost souls.

Alison intercepted him just before he could vanish into the world outside of the office. "Ian!" she called, jogging up, cheeks pink.

He raised a hand in weary greeting.

"Missed you yesterday," she said, smiling brightly. "Got any tips on multivariate testing?"

Ian blinked.

"A/B splits," he said automatically. "Get everything on a spreadsheet. Only one test at a time. Keep it boring."

Alison laughed, a little breathlessly. "You're wasted here, Ian."

He shrugged. "Story of my life."

She watched him walk away, something wistful – or calculating – flickering behind her eyes. *Surely, she didn't find him attractive*, Ian mused as he tossed a lazy over-the-shoulder wave. "Off to a meeting!" he called.

Nobody questioned it.

That was the trick. Look useless enough, and people stopped worrying about what you are up to. Ian had it down to fine art!

Ian walked briskly down City Road towards the Bank of England, the air sharp with diesel and ambition. The city blurred around him. Glass towers, honking vans, the unbothered whirl of a busy capital – racing along in the pursuit of mammon.

But then, as if someone had pressed pause, he stepped off the pavement and into a sliver of forgotten time.

The seedy, downtrodden launderette was where he often met Griffin for briefings.

Ancient. Yellowing. Somehow both damp and over-dry. The windows were fogged with years of steam and half-evaporated lives. A fluorescent tube above the door buzzed with the slow death-rattle of a lightbulb that should've been replaced during the Blair administration. Inside, the place smelled of damp socks, overused detergent, and quiet despair. Washing machines rattled like arthritic bones. Tumble dryers churned with the grace of a cement mixer. Somewhere, someone's zip clattered endlessly against the drum, like a large fly banging at a double-glazed window.

An elderly woman in a fleece jacket sat near the front, hunched over a copy of *Chat* magazine, her mouth pursed like she was reading something obscene. A plastic bag rustled at her feet, filled with unmatched socks and unopened pork pies.

Ian ducked his head and stepped inside, weaving past laundry baskets that dripped with questionable moisture.

In the far corner, hunched at a metal table, stood Griffin, folding towels like he'd been trained to fold army parachutes.

Compact, powerful, and carved from some dark weatherproof and bulletproof material no longer found in modern soldiers, Griffin had deep brown eyes that didn't miss much and a faint white scar that ran like a crack in porcelain from his temple to the edge of his jaw. His black hair was clipped short – military short – and flecked with grey at the temples. He wore an old green parka, unzipped at the throat to reveal a faded regimental T-shirt and a leather cord bearing an antique kukri pendant – a nod to what he used to be, and what he could still become if you gave him reason.

Ex-Gurkha.

Now MI5's quiet fixer.

The sort of man who didn't carry a weapon because he could turn a pencil into one.

The sort of man you didn't notice until you were already dying – or dead!

Ian approached slowly.

"You still wear that tie in public?" Griffin asked, eyes never leaving the towel in his hands.

Ian looked down at the abomination knotted around his collar – a wide, grease-splotched relic from the 90s that may once have featured cartoon ducks but now mostly resembled forensic evidence to some dark crime.

"It's a statement piece," Ian said cheerfully. "Like a Tracey Emin."

Griffin didn't smile. Just snorted softly and handed him a battered brown dossier from beneath a neatly folded pile of bath sheets.

"High-level contract," he muttered. "Iranian intelligence officer. Tehran's own spook whisperer. Coming in next week under diplomatic smokescreen. Nasty piece of work. Very dangerous"

Ian flipped the folder open.

The photograph inside was printed on matte paper, slightly creased. A middle-aged man in a navy suit, slicked-back hair, too-white teeth. Wealthy, cocky, used to surviving things he shouldn't. Ian studied it for three seconds, committing everything.

"Standard cut-out?" he asked, already flicking to the logistics.

"Unconfirmed," Griffin replied. "No footprint yet. We're offering three million. Half up front. Do it clean. No splash."

Ian nodded.

"Cover?"

"Hotel staff," Griffin said, folding a T-shirt with precision that bordered on surgical. "Westminster Radisson. Concierge crew. Arrives Wednesday night, checking in under an EU conference pseudonym. You'll be on the shift."

Ian closed the file with a soft thwap, the weight of it tucked under one arm.

"Consider it sorted," he said.

Griffin didn't look up. Just kept folding. "You've got forty-eight hours. Don't cock it up."

Ian gave him a thin smile and backed out of the launderette, the door jangling softly behind him. Back outside, the city resumed – loud, fast, glassy. Inside the launderette, the old woman continued to turn pages. And Griffin folded another towel, like he was prepping for war.

Instead of walking back to his office, he took a long circuitous route through several cobble stoned back streets and then a quick, short cut through a big public house – in the front slowly, out the back quickly. To throw off anyone trying to follow him. Until he arrived at a luxurious apartment block that glistened with the smell of discrete old money and inter-generational wealth.

Before entering, Ian double checked yet again that he hadn't been followed. Then he entered the large, state of the art revolving doors into a world of lavish luxury and utter comfort.

The marble floors of the lobby gleamed like wet ice.

Ian nodded at the doorman – a subtle, almost imperceptible nod – and slipped into the private lift, up to the top floor penthouse. The doors whispered shut behind him.

Inside the mirrored walls of the elevator, his reflection straightened. Tie already removed, jacket shrugged off, grubby Post Office worker no more. Something brand new.

When the lift doors opened, Ian Taylor stepped into a completely different world. Yet he appeared as at home here as he did back at his slightly shabby family home in North London.

The penthouse didn't look like it belonged to the Ian Taylor of North London. Which, of course, was the point.

It was the kind of building you only noticed when you were looking for somewhere to hide twenty million pounds.

Inside the apartment, it was still. Perfectly still. The floors were black-stained oak, polished to a soft sheen that swallowed noise. The air smelled faintly of sandalwood and money – the expensive kind, not the gaudy, Dubai-on-a-budget kind. Every corner had been designed for silence, discretion and utility: recessed lighting, floor-to-ceiling windows softened with discreet steel-mesh blinds and walls the colour of a mild nervous breakdown – calm, tasteful, forgettable.

The living area was an ode to masculine understatement. Two dark leather armchairs, brutal in shape but soft to the touch, sat opposite a low coffee table made from reclaimed aircraft aluminium. On it: a stack of clean-sleeved dossiers, a glass ashtray the size of a hubcap, and a single Montblanc fountain pen. To the left, a built-in bar glowed under low lighting: crystal decanters of whisky so old they predated mobile phones, and a locked drawer with a small vial of cyanide nestled between two bottles of ancient bourbon. A leather humidor held cigars more expensive than a good night out at a Michelin star restaurant, each one tagged and humidified with more care than Ian gave his own teeth. Behind a seemingly ordinary mirror – fingerprint-locked, pressure-sensitive – lay the truth of this oasis of calm and sophistication.

The mirrored panel hissed open to reveal a hidden armoury, even more extensive than the one in Ian's back garden shed – elegant and obscene.

Inside: rows of custom handguns, high powered rifles, knives balanced like surgical instruments, micro-gadgets, fake passports, millions in cash, in six major currencies, and a disguise kit that included everything from latex masks to teeth whitening strips. A dozen tailored suits hung in chromatic order, all immaculately pressed – many of them monogrammed. A silent cashmere army waiting to be deployed.

The wardrobe across the bedroom housed more than clothing. It contained a cornucopia of luxurious secrets. A silk-lined box held half a dozen luxury watches – not all for timekeeping, but for detonating, decoding, distracting. One drawer was devoted entirely to contact lenses in various colours, another to cufflinks, two of which contained injectable venom. Even the bookshelves were a lie. Hardcovers hollowed out to hide burner phones, encrypted drives, antique lockpicks. The collected works of Graham Greene had never been read – but they had helped extract a diplomat at very short notice from a sticky situation in Kiev back in 2014.

The kitchen, rarely used, looked like a glossy magazine spread: matte black fittings, copper taps, an oven that could autoclave evidence if required.

Only the bathroom betrayed a hint of indulgence: a rainfall shower big enough to host a small diplomatic summit, and towels thick enough to smother a medium-sized informant.

It was a place of discipline. Precision. Quiet power. Which was why Ian, even as he walked across its expensive floors and poured himself 35-year-old Glenfiddich into a hand-cut crystal glass, still felt slightly out of place – like he'd burgled someone else's home and was waiting to be caught by a better version of himself. Still, it was his. And when the job called for control, for quiet, for clean kills and no questions...

this was where Ian Taylor lived. Or at least – the part of him that knew how to disappear.

Ian stripped out of his grubby office day clothes, tossing them into a stainless-steel clothes hamper. He stepped into the walk-in wet room, steaming the grime of suburbia off his skin. Dirt, smells, stains and fragments of food fell away and were whisked down the drain, disappearing like a clown's make up.

When he emerged, he was a very different creature altogether: silk shirt, sharp trousers, kid leather shoes, so soft they barely whispered against the floor.

He poured himself another large Scotch, lit a cigar, and settled into a chair with the dossier. A Great White Shark, slipping into deeper waters, searching for its prey.

Ian dialled home, holding the phone closely to his right ear and his whisky to his left. "Hey Mummy," he said, slipping into domestic cadence. "Something's come up. Might be a bit late tonight."

Susan's voice floated back, calm, a little distant. "Oh... okay. That's fine. I think I might go to the gym."

Ian froze, Scotch halfway to his lips. "The gym?"

"Yes. Why not?"

A long beat.

He sensed something... off. But not enough to act. "Well... have fun," he said finally.

Susan chuckled. "You too, Daddy."

The line went dead.

Ian stared at the phone for a long moment. Then drained the Scotch in a single glug. It was now time to take a look at the Radison Hotel, where Ian had been contracted to kill the senior Iranian operative.

The Westminster Radisson didn't scream luxury. It whispered it – with manicured discretion and the quiet confidence of a place that didn't need to prove anything. From the outside, it was a glass-and-stone monolith, its branding minimal, its doormen sculpted out of calm confidence and posture. The lobby glowed with that soft golden hue expensive lighting consultants referred to as "trustworthy opulence." Italian marble underfoot. High-backed chairs no one ever actually sat in. A scent in the air – subtle, chemical, something like expensive oranges.

But Ian didn't enter through the front. He went in around the back, behind a loading bay that reeked of old oil, bin juice, and brake dust, the glamour peeled away.

The service entrance was a metal fire door, propped open with a greasy crate. The floor was slick in patches with something that probably wasn't water. The air buzzed with fluorescent lights and bad temper.

Ian moved through it all like he'd been born there. Now wearing cleaner's overalls – that he had slipped over his underclothes - slightly too tight. Fake ID badge clipped at a slant. Clipboard in hand. He walked like he belonged: brisk, unimpressed, avoiding eye contact but scanning everything. Pipes ran above the ceiling panels like arteries. Staff lockers lined one wall, dented and tagged with stickers. Somewhere nearby, a dishwasher groaned under the weight of a thousand crusted ramekins.

The service corridors twisted in labyrinthine fashion – narrow, beige-painted arteries threading through the guts of the hotel. Pale grey carpet, thin and fraying at the edges, sucked sound out of footsteps. There were signs everywhere: CATERING, MAINTENANCE, DELIVERIES, and arrows that pointed in two directions at once.

Ian passed a housekeeping trolley abandoned against the wall, its contents spilling out like entrails – folded towels, half-used soaps, toilet roll shaped into a pointless origami triangle.

He rounded a corner. Stopped.

Another cleaner stood in the corridor, facing him. Male. Mid-thirties. Middle Eastern. His uniform was the same as Ian's – identical, in fact, down to the slightly frayed hems and the same laminated badge with a forged staff number.

Their eyes locked. Just for a second. A flicker of something passed between them – not alarm, not hostility, but something cold and technical. Mutual assessment.

Ian clocked the posture first: too good for hotel work. Back straight, head still, shoulders square. A man trained to move quietly, to handle stress, to calculate. Then the eyes: too alert. Scanning, sharp. Like he wasn't seeing Ian so much as triangulating him. He wasn't a cleaner. And Ian wasn't either.

Both of them knew it.

A heartbeat stretched long and thin.

Recognition – not of face, but of type.

Then, wordlessly, they stepped past one another. No nod. No threat. No fake smile. Just two ghosts moving through the same haunted place.

As Ian walked on, clipboard swinging loosely in one hand, he didn't look back. He didn't have to. He already knew that whatever this hotel's public face was selling – trust, discretion, comfort – its back rooms were bristling with secrets.

He made his way up two flights using the service stairs – scuffed lino, fire exit maps yellowing under cracked plastic – and paused outside Room 1106.

It was quiet up here. Mid-tier executive floor. Not the kind of room a head of state would book, but not exactly a Travelodge either.

Ian checked the corridor. Clear.

He took out the spare keycard – lifted earlier from housekeeping's central lock-box – and slid it home in one fluid motion.

Green light. Soft click.

He was in.

The air inside the freshly turned-out room smelled faintly of bleach and orange blossom – the standard Radisson cocktail. Neat lines. Folded towels. A bed made with taut precision, as if the chambermaid had graduated from Sandhurst.

Ian moved like a man doing inventory. Calm. Clinical. He unscrewed the back of the wall-mounted smoke detector, slipped in a pinhead mic. He then wired the bedside lamp with an electromagnetic pickup. Planted a contact-mic under the desk drawer, and a tiny wide-angle lens behind the TV screen, facing the bed. All in less than three minutes.

No wasted movement.

No fingerprints.

No noise.

He'd just finished checking the toilet cistern – a favoured hiding place for backup comms units and cyanide capsules – when something stopped him in his tracks. A feeling. That little itch behind the eyes. He froze. Looked again.

The phone on the bedside table wasn't the usual cheap plastic job. It was a VOIP-capable model – slightly newer. Switched off at the wall. Odd. He pulled it closer. Flipped it. Underneath: a wafer-thin film of duct tape, almost invisible. Tucked beneath that – an RFID tag the size of a fingernail. Not hotel issue. He checked the lamp again. Carefully. There, inside the base: a laser-drilled hole the size of a pinhead. Optical feed.

Someone had already bugged the room.

Ian stepped back, slowly.

So. Either the Iranians had pre-wired their own room. Or someone else was planning to listen in on the Iranian too.

Or both.

He took out his encrypted phone. Snapped a photo of the tag, the optical hole, the phone base. Then, carefully, he glanced around the room one final time.

Still pristine.

Still hotel perfect.

And now, deeply compromised.

\*\*\*

As Ian arrived home later that night his battered leather shoes crunched onto the gravel driveway. The house glowed warm and yellow behind net curtains.

Safe. Ordinary. Forgettable.

He stepped inside, shedding the city and the luxury of his penthouse apartment like an old skin. He found his wife up in the bedroom.

Susan was radiant, fresh from the shower, hair wrapped in a towel.

"Gym was great," she said, smiling over her mug of tea, eyes sparkling, face glowing. "I think I might start going every day," she continued.

Ian stiffened slightly. "Every day?" he asked.

Susan nodded. "I need a little... change," she said hesitantly.

Tolstoy watched Ian from his corner, one ear twitching.

Ian nodded slowly.

Change. That most dangerous of words.

Later that night, Susan lay beside him, breathing slow and steady.

Ian stared at the ceiling, wide awake. He reached out, brushed her arm lightly – friendly. "Night, night, Mummy," he whispered.

"Night," she murmured impersonally back, without turning.

Tolstoy remained at the foot of the bed, eyes open, unblinking.

Once Ian was certain everyone in the house was completely asleep, he got up in his stained striped pyjamas and made for the shed – wearing his favourite pair of gardening slippers.

In the dark, Ian powered up the secure phone. He typed:
*Need to investigate another potential FOX locally. Require Company van – decorator style to provide cover. Tomorrow morning if possible.*

He hit SEND.

The reply blinked back almost immediately:

*Request logged. Stand by.*

Ian locked the shed behind him and stared out into the suburban darkness before returning to his bed and snoring wife.

Something was happening.

And Ian Taylor – suburban fool, corporate embarrassment, silent killer – would be ready.

Chapter Three
# No Smoke Without Fire

*"Trust no one. Not even the dog. Especially the dog."*
**~ Redacted field notes, author unknown**

# Chapter 3

# No Smoke Without Fire

In Ian Taylor's experience, nothing good ever came after the words, "I'm just popping out." It was the kind of phrase that presaged disaster – a car crash, a lost dog, an affair, or even worse – a dinner party.

He watched from the bed as Susan finished tying on her trainers, stuffing a towel into her sports bag with determined optimism.

"I'm popping out – shopping, then the gym," she said breezily.

Ian, now half-dressed and bleary-eyed, squinted at her like she'd announced she was joining the Foreign Legion. "Gym again?" he said, trying for casual and failing.

Susan tried not to rise to it. "Yes, Daddy. Don't look so surprised."

"No, no," Ian said, forcing a smile. "Good for you. Pump it up."

Susan kissed him briskly on the forehead and swept out of the room before he could muster a better line.

He heard the front door slam, the rev of her Honda's engine, and the squeal of tyres as she screeched off without so much as a backward glance.

Ian sat on the edge of the bed, hurt blooming quietly in his chest.

Tolstoy lifted his massive head from the floor and regarded him solemnly.

"Right," Ian muttered. "Enough, is enough!" He thumbed the worn keys of the house phone, dialling Ruth, his boss at work without much hope.

Ruth's clipped tones answered on the first ring.

"Ian, where the hell are -"

"Hi Ruth, rough night. I won't be in today," Ian said, curtly cutting her off, bulldozing her objections. "I'll send Alison the spreadsheet she needs to make sure the mailing goes out on time. She knows what to do. Thanks. Bye." He hung up before she could argue.

Efficiency.

He now needed to prepare.

The shed sat at the bottom of the garden like it had always been there – squat, crooked, unremarkable. The roof sagged slightly, the windows were mottled with age, and the door groaned like an old man being asked to stand up too quickly.

To the casual observer, it was exactly what it looked like: a place for rusted tools, abandoned flowerpots, maybe a lawnmower if you were lucky.

But Ian Taylor had never been a casual anything.

He stepped inside, ducking slightly to avoid the low beam, and locked the door behind him with a quiet, deliberate click.

The smell hit him first – a familiar cocktail of oil, dust, and something faintly metallic that clung to the air like memory. Years of grease and gun oil, buried under the surface of half a dozen fake tins of Cuprinol and a half-built birdhouse he'd once used to smuggle an encrypted SIM card to someone in Tower Hamlets.

Light filtered through a single grimy skylight, slicing the gloom into pale beams that lit up particles of dust and the occasional drifting cobweb.

He crossed to the back wall, reached behind a shelf stacked with cracked terracotta pots, and pressed three fingers against an innocuous-looking knot in the wood.

With a soft hiss, a section of the panelling swung open, revealing the truth. Behind the pegboard and shelves of old WD-40 cans, the shed's heart ticked away like a clockwork assassin.

Inside the concealed compartment were rows of neatly stacked equipment. Quiet. Deadly. Ordered with the kind of obsessive neatness Ian rarely applied to the rest of his life.

He scanned the contents like a man picking tools for an awkward bit of plumbing – only this job required fewer spanners and more plausible deniability.

From the left-hand shelf, he pulled a pair of battered overalls – flecked with dried paint, smeared with dust, the knees reinforced with inconspicuous Kevlar panels. The kind decorators wore after twenty years of backbreaking domestic service. Or at least, the kind they should have worn if they were expecting small arms fire.

Next, he selected a coiled fibre optic snake cam – neatly wound, lens polished bright and clear, its cable wound in a perfect figure-eight. Useful for peering through air vents, keyholes, or under suspicious floorboards. Or just watching your wife's gym session from the rafters, depending on how your day was going.

From the central drawer came two Karambit knives – twin black arcs of steel, curved like the claws of something that wasn't meant to be tamed. Ian weighed them briefly in his hands, then sheathed them into the leather pockets sewn just behind each thigh – designed for the job.

Two compact pistols followed, discreet and silenced, tucked into the dual holsters hidden beneath the overalls' outer shell. Lightweight. Familiar. Comforting.

A battered green thermos came next – faded branding, dented rim, lots of paint. It had once belonged to a Royal Mail courier, now long retired or possibly buried. Inside the flask: a heady mix of hot coffee laced with whisky. Field fuel.

Finally, for appearances, he tossed in a bundle of paintbrushes – the cheap kind with stiff bristles and dried white gloss clogging the handles. They looked the part and could always be used to flick ammonia into someone's eyes at close range, if it came to that.

Ian stepped back and checked his gear. Nothing flashy. Nothing stupid. Just the basics.

Then he zipped the paint spattered overalls halfway, strapped on the gear under the loose fabric, and turned to Tolstoy, who was sitting patiently on the threshold, his massive black bulk blotting out the daylight like a night club bouncer.

"Right," Ian muttered, tightening the zip. "Time to find out what's really going on at that bloody gym."

Tolstoy thumped his tail against the floorboards once – in a flash of emphatic approval. Ian walked outside his front door looking every bit the seasoned house professional decorator. The street was quiet, mid-morning lull in full swing.

A white van screeched around the corner and jerked to a halt outside Ian's house. The side read: JONES & SON – PAINTERS & DECORATORS. A tribute to the long-standing British tradition of lying to strangers via signage.

Jim leaned out the driver's window, grinning like a man who found chaos inherently funny. "Nice disguise," he said.

Ian jogged over, Tolstoy at his heels. "Cheers, Jim," he said, slinging his kit into the back. "Something's not right. There's something off at that gym."

Jim shrugged. "Your gut's never wrong."

Ian paused, considered, then broke wind loudly and wafted the smell toward his own nose with his hand.

Jim gagged theatrically and cranked down the window.

"See? Highly calibrated," Ian said proudly, settling down into his seat in van while adjusting his outfit and making a few changes to his clothing, as Jim drove, which involved him having to half strip off and get redressed again.

Getting changed in a moving van was an exercise in balance and hypermobility. Ian pulled his battered overalls back on with the grace of a drunk octopus. He re-holstered the knives and pistols back inside his hidden pockets, adjusted the fibre cam's case, and checked the battered thermos flask for... motivational fluid – swigging frantically.

Jim watched from the corner of his eye, amused. "Blimey. That's some serious decorator's kit."

"When it comes to family," Ian said solemnly, "I get *very* serious." He swigged from the flask.

"Scotch?" Jim guessed.

"Irish!" Ian corrected with wounded pride.

They soon arrived at the gym, driving up into the carpark next to the building next door. The gym squatted at the end of a row of drab warehouses, pretending to be more glamorous than it was.

***

It loomed across the car park: a squat two-storey building with smoked glass windows and motivational slogans painted in aggressive typefaces.

'NO EXCUSES.'

'ONE MORE REP.'

'BECOME YOUR BEST SELF.'

It had the cheerful brutality of a place where people screamed at kettlebells and pretended pain was personal growth.

Ian leaned forward, scanning the place through smudged a pair of Ray-Bans he'd found in a glovebox years ago. He looked less like a covert operative and more like someone who might do unspeakable things to your window frames with a tin of white high gloss. "She's not here yet," he muttered. "Silver car, blue gym bag, top knot like a pastry swirl. Not arrived."

Jim arched an eyebrow. "You always describe your wife like a dessert?"

"Only when I'm worried about her," Ian replied grimly.

He reached into the back, grabbing the old metal toolbox with chipped red paint. Inside: the usual selection of brushes, scrapers, and putty knives – all real, all dull –layered over a false bottom that held wire cutters, a tracking device, a collapsible baton, and a snub-nosed pistol and a hypodermic full of powerful tranquiliser.

Jim cranked the window open and leaned away from Ian with theatrical disgust.

"Christ. What is that smell?"

"Field-tested disguise," Ian said proudly, adjusting the waistband of his overalls. "It's a cologne called Brico Dépôt. With notes of sweat, despair, and creosote."

Jim laughed and said, "Decorators get all the perks."

Ian reached under his seat and pulled on a pair of paint-flecked gloves; fingers worn down to show just enough skin to prove authenticity and previous use. He checked his reflection in the cracked wing mirror of the van: hair flattened under a baseball cap with a long-faded Screwfix logo, a smear of something suspicious across his cheek, and the beginnings of a hunch that suggested decades of stairwells and ignored invoices.

"Alright," he said. "I'm going up."

Jim nodded and tilted his seat back. "I'll keep watch. If you're not back in an hour, I'm selling your dog to the Russians."

"Don't joke. They'd promote him straight to colonel and then throw him off a hotel balcony."

Ian popped the door open and stepped out, toolbox and toolbelt in hand, moving with the slow-footed heaviness of a man paid by the hour.

"Time to redecorate," he said, setting the ladder against the side of the building, and climbing carefully up the ladder, toolbelt now hanging from his belt, banging against his hip. At the upper floor, he balanced precariously, slipped two fibre-optic snake cams through a gap in the office window, and activated the feed on his tiny handheld monitor.

At last, Susan arrived at the gym with a squeal of tyres and loud music on her radio – parking directly in front of the front doors. The doors of the gym hissed open with a faint hydraulic sigh – the kind of overly dramatic entrance usually reserved for dental clinics or Bond villains.

Susan stepped inside, flushed, strands of hair escaping her ponytail in soft wisps. She wore black Lycra leggings and a fitted hoodie, her sports bag slung casually over one shoulder – an expensive one Ian didn't recognise. She paused just beyond the entrance mat, catching her breath, cheeks pink with cold and something else. Nerves, maybe.

Ian, watching from his perch through the fibre optic lens, felt a flicker of something unhelpfully human tighten across his chest. He was starting to get angry. Then he saw the trainer come to greet her. He had clearly been expecting her.

The man emerged from a side corridor with the casual confidence of someone who had never once doubted the perfection of his own reflection. Mid-thirties, tall, built like a fire door with limbs – the kind of muscle you had to work very hard to pretend was natural. His blonde hair was cut in a tight military fade, skin tanned just enough to suggest beach holidays and dubious protein powders. His gym polo top was three sizes too tight and damp in all the wrong places.

The smile he gave Susan was just shy of predatory.

"There you are," he said, accent Eastern European – possibly Bulgarian. "Thought you weren't coming."

Susan gave a sheepish smile, brushing a strand of hair behind her ear. "Just running late. It's been... one of those mornings." Her voice was light, casual – but Ian knew her cadence too well. A touch too bright. A little forced.

The trainer's eyes roved for half a second longer than they should have. His grin widened, sharklike.

"No problem," he said smoothly. "Come on. We'll warm up upstairs." He gestured toward the stairs and turned with the confidence of a man who expected to be followed.

Susan did.

As they passed the front desk, their arms brushed – a subtle moment that might have been nothing. Might have been everything. She didn't pull away.

Ian adjusted the camera, zooming in, the feed twitching faintly with motion blur. He felt the pulse in his neck climb half a beat.

The trainer was saying something now – something low, his hand hovering near the small of Susan's back.

Ian didn't need the audio. He'd seen all this before. Ian switched cameras to the office area where they were now headed.

The office was small and badly lit, a half-hearted attempt at professionalism tucked into the upstairs corner of the gym. A thin strip of brown carpet – worn flat in the middle – stretched between a battered desk and two aluminium filing cabinets that leaned slightly toward each other, like co-conspirators. The blinds were drawn, half-cocked, one of them bent as though someone had punched it in frustration at some stage.

A motivational poster hung crooked on the wall. It featured a man with glistening abs sprinting through fake fog beneath bold lettering that read: 'BE YOUR OWN HERO.' There was a crack through the top left corner, a diagonal fracture that split the hero's face in two.

Ian's camera lens adjusted for the dim light, the image stuttering faintly as it focused. Susan stood just inside the room, shifting her weight from foot to foot. Her shoulders were slightly hunched, sports bag still slung on one arm. The flush from her walk had faded. Now she just looked uncertain.

The trainer closed the door behind her with a soft click.

For a moment, they both stood there in silence.

Then he stepped closer and kissed her boldly. It wasn't a passing kiss. Not a hesitant, what-if sort of peck. It lingered – two full seconds too long – his fingers brushing lightly through her hair like it was a habit, like he'd imagined doing it enough times that the gesture had already worn a groove in his brain.

Susan pulled back first, blinking, flustered. Her hand came up between them as if to reset the air.

"Steady," she said, half-laughing. "I'm married."

The trainer didn't flinch.

"So am I," he replied with an easy shrug, like they were trading marital stats on a game show. He reached out and brushed her arm with the backs of his fingers – soft, slow. "But I can't stop thinking of you."

Susan's smile faltered. Not gone, not yet — but flickering at the edges.

"I do like you..." she said quietly. "But I also love my husband." It was a line. A boundary. Polite. Final.

But he wasn't listening. He laughed – low and soft, the kind of laugh that only pretended to be charming. "You don't have to choose," he murmured, stepping closer, hand resting lightly at her waist now. "Just a bit of fun. Come on. You know you want this. You've been flirting with me all week."

He nudged her back toward the desk, pressure light but firm and deliberate.

Ian gripped the ladder outside, knuckles whitening, the metal cold and rough beneath his gloves.

Inside the room, Susan's body language changed in a heartbeat. Her back stiffened. Her arm locked out to keep him away.

"Get off me," she said, sharply now – not laughing anymore.

But he didn't move.

Outside, a strong gust of wind caught the ladder Ian was standing on and rattled it violently against the building. Ian flattened himself to the wall, heart suddenly hammering. He felt angry. Very angry!

Inside, the trainer hesitated – just for a split second – distracted by the noise of the ladder.

That was all she needed. Susan shoved him back. Hard. He staggered back into the edge of the desk, clipping it with his hip.

Before he could recover, she was already at the door, yanking it open, slipping into the corridor with rapid, increasingly furious steps.

The trainer didn't follow. He just stood there, rubbing his hip, expression unreadable.

Susan soon burst out of the front entrance, chest heaving.

Ian ducked his head instinctively, shielding his face.

"Good girl," Ian muttered to himself, feeling increasingly relieved yet still very angry. He slid down the ladder faster than a man his size had any right to, landing with a grunt. He didn't look back.

Ian changed into a new disguise, in the back of the van, and set up nearby under a set of railway arches, where the main path from the gym and the nearest high street ran, to see if he could intercept the trainer.

The railway arches had once been built for utility, not beauty – great sweeping curves of soot-streaked brick, laid in the era of steam and empire, now half-swallowed by urban decay. The brickwork sweated with condensation in the evenings, the mortar permanently damp, as if the city itself was exhaling something it didn't want to keep.

The arches stood along a forgotten stretch of back road behind Finsbury Park, a place where streetlights flickered and the pavement was a patchwork of old chewing gum, puddled oil, and bottle caps flattened by delivery vans. Discarded takeaway boxes fluttered in the wind like wilted origami. A broken mattress leaned against a wall, its springs exposed like so many snapped ribs.

Above, trains roared past at intervals, their sound muffled by years of grime. Every few minutes, a dull rumble would roll through the arches – not enough to make you jump, just enough to remind you that the world was still moving, even if you weren't.

Beneath Arch 14 – partially obscured by graffiti and a forgotten charity furniture drop – Ian Taylor set up his station.

A battered chestnut roaster, the kind that might once have seen action on a winter market stall, wheezed into reluctant life. Its blackened sides bore the scorch marks of a thousand overcooked attempts. He struck the ignition with practiced care, adjusting the vent to produce just the right plume of fragrant, nutty smoke – enough to lend the scene a kind of credibility, not so much inviting as tolerating.

Next came the blanket – thin, frayed at the corners, and stained with things best left unexamined. Ian spread it across the concrete with deliberate care, weighting the corners with old bricks and a half-empty sack of coal.

Tolstoy padded in behind him, nails clicking faintly on the concrete. The dog didn't bark, didn't whine – just circled once and flopped beside Ian's setup with the ease of a veteran. A giant Russian Black Terrier with the expression of a war poet and the breath of a long-dead saint, Tolstoy was the perfect co-conspirator.

Ian pulled a grimy wool cap low over his brow – the kind that looked like it had soaked up a decade's worth of sad news and spilled gravy. Underneath, he let his face go slack, let his posture sag. His shoulders slumped; his chest hollowed. His movements lost that economy of trained efficiency.

Now, he was just another piece of the scenery. His clothes – baggy, layered, stained – completed the picture. His trousers had multiple knee patches. His coat was corduroy and smelled faintly of pickled onions and mothballs. One of his boots had a tongue that refused to stay inside, giving him a permanent lopsided gait.

He took out a chipped enamel mug, filled it halfway with lukewarm instant coffee, then added a glug from a small hip flask. He sipped, winced theatrically, and coughed once for good measure.

Now, he didn't look like a threat. He looked like a man who had lost everything except a bad smell and a big dog. Perfect.

Above, another train rumbled over the tracks, the noise vibrating through the bones of the city. Ian didn't even blink. He leaned back against the brick, let the shadows do their work, and waited. Then all of a sudden, out of the blue, the philandering Trainer strolled by, phone out, oblivious.

Ian beckoned lazily.

"How much for a bag of them?" the Trainer said, nodding at the chestnuts.

"First one's free," Ian said, and then jabbed the syringe straight into the Trainer's neck with clinical precision.

The man sagged instantly, a dead weight. Ian caught him under the arms and hauled him up behind a builder's skip.

Tolstoy trotted after Ian, tail wagging.

The Trainer was out cold, slumped like a broken marionette under the glow of a flickering wall light, his limbs arranged unceremoniously on the damp concrete like someone had dropped a man-shaped sack of gym memberships.

Ian knelt beside him with the focus of a man laying out a picnic, slipping on a pair of thin black nitrile gloves one finger at a time. He moved without hurry, every motion deliberate – the sort of calm that made people nervous in operating theatres and war zones.

From inside Ian's weathered toolbox came a small, zippered leather roll full of surgical knives. He unwrapped it gently, like a chef preparing his knives ready to prepare for service. Inside: a selection of gleaming steel – honed, balanced, quietly terrible. He selected a compact, curved blade with a ribbed grip and a hooked tip, wiped it with an alcohol pad, and held it briefly to the light. Then, with a final glance at the still-sedated trainer – now stirring faintly – Ian got to work.

No noise. No flourish. Just steady hands and old, ugly skill.

He pulled down the Trainer's track suit bottoms and started to cut. He cut with the quiet focus of a field medic, not out of cruelty, but out of a long-settled pragmatism. The blade was sharp, the cuts clean, precise. It took less than thirty seconds. Blood welled and steamed in the cool air.

The trainer twitched once, then fell limp again – once again unconscious. His genitalia completely surgically removed! *He wouldn't be dabbling in another man's pond again,* Ian thought to himself!

Ian reached out to the old chestnut roaster beside him, where a metal scoop was glowing softly in the heat – its handle wrapped in cloth, its edge radiating a quiet, menacing heat. He cauterised the wound with one clean sizzle.

There was a hiss like bacon on a pan and the sudden, unmistakable smell of seared meat. The air filled with it – thick, metallic, curdled with something bitter. Ian then started to cook the removed rubbery flesh package.

Tolstoy, who had been lying quietly a few feet away, lifted his great head and gave a low, interested whine. His ears perked. His nostrils flared.

"Patience, lad," Ian murmured, not looking up. "Let 'em cook."

He took the severed genitals and skewered them onto the roasting prongs, rotating them over the open flame with slow, deliberate care – the same way he might have turned a marshmallow.

The meat sizzled, curled. A few drops of fat popped against the heat. When they were fully cooked through – crisped around the edges, no rawness left – Ian tipped them off the end of the prong with a gentle flick.

Tolstoy caught them mid-air with a single smooth chomp.

This was no ordinary snack.

He chewed with the placid joy of a dog who did not question providence, only accepted it. His tail thumped against the floor, a low, steady, repetitive beat of approval.

Ian peeled off his gloves with a snap and dropped them into the metal burn-can beside him. He reached for his hip flask, swirled it, and took a short pull.

"Waste not," he muttered, wiping his hands on a rag. "Want not."

Then he looked over at the still-twitching trainer and gave a small nod.

"You'll live. Which is more than you deserve."

\*\*\*

Jim drove up, humming tunelessly, while Ian lounged in the passenger seat, scrubbed clean and changed into fresh clothes.

"So…did you kill him?" Jim asked casually.

Ian shook his head. "No. Just gave him a bit of a bollocking."

Jim snorted and flicked on the comms to MI5 HQ.

"Got a bloke under the arches. Serious assault. Enraged husband maybe. Let's build a backstory."

Ian grinned. "I *was* bloody enraged."

"Never rub another man's rhubarb," Jim said solemnly.

They both burst out laughing.

Jim dropped both Ian and Tolstoy at the top of Ian's road. Ian quickly jumped into the back of the van to change into his normal clothes and asked Jim to get the disguises cleaned for him and returned to the garden shed.

The sunset smeared blood-red across the sky. Ian strolled home, Tolstoy loping beside him, both radiating innocent contentment as if nothing unusual had happened.

Susan was in the kitchen, chopping vegetables with fierce concentration.

Ian leaned in the doorway. "Hello Mummy. Good time at the gym?"

Susan paused, glanced at him sideways.

"Erm... no. Didn't go in the end. Not really my bag I've decided."

"Oh?"

"The owner's a bit...well...creepy to be honest."

Ian smiled. "I'm glad. I'd hate to lose you to some good-looking muscle-bound freak."

Susan snorted nervously. "Don't be silly, Daddy. No chance of that. I only want you."

Tolstoy burped a big meaty burp with a guilty look in his eyes. Susan wafted the air furiously, laughing despite herself. Some things – the best things – didn't need to change after all she decided.

Chapter Four
# Daddy Issues

*"Surprise is the most underrated weapon in the kitchen."*
**~ MI5 Internal Memo: Improvised Close-Quarters Tools**

## Chapter 4

# Daddy Issues

There are breakfasts that nourish the body, and breakfasts that offend basic human decency. Ian Taylor's creation this particular morning fell firmly into the second category.

At the kitchen counter, he assembled his masterpiece with grim enthusiasm:

A scoop of slightly stale granola.

A dusting of cornflakes.

A dollop – no, an industrialised *slab* – of Greek yoghurt.

Sliced banana, slapped on like a pile of bricks.

And, for good measure, a crumbled handful of salt and vinegar crisps, sprinkled with the flourish of a Michelin chef suffering a psychotic episode.

Daisy and Max both sat at the table, transfixed by the horror unfolding.

Ian admired his handiwork, then turned with a proud grin. "I'm having the healthy option today," he announced. "Gotta keep up with all those hunks up Mummy's gym!"

Susan entered just in time to catch the last part, her cheeks flushing pink. "I told you," she said hurriedly, waving a hand as if swatting the idea away, "I'm not going up the gym anymore. It's full of predatory men."

Daisy raised an eyebrow. "You should go and take Dad. He might get fit. Or at least slightly less spherical."

Susan, panicking slightly, jumped in. "Oh, I don't think your father would like my gym, darling. It's not really… well, erm, his vibe."

Ian puffed out his chest proudly. "I'm already a titan of a man!" he declared. "I could take down those plastic musclemen with my tiny pinky," he announced proudly.

He wiggled the offending finger at the breakfast table, which – covered in crushed crisps and yoghurt splashes – looked like it had witnessed a particularly dramatic explosion.

Daisy muttered under her breath, "Tosser."

Tolstoy, ever loyal, sat beneath the counter, gazing up at Ian like he was the second coming of Christ.

Ian beamed, scooping up a massive spoonful of his monstrosity and wolfing it down with a grotesque slurp. Crumbs, flakes, and yoghurt sprayed across the counter like a Jackson Pollock painting in edible form.

He finished the entire bowl in record time, leaned back, and belched so loudly the cutlery rattled in the drawer. "Right, I'm off to work. See you all tonight, my darlings," Ian said cheerfully, getting up, wiping his mouth on his sleeve. "Don't do anything I wouldn't do."

"We wouldn't do anything you would do," Max shouted after him.

He kissed Susan's forehead with exaggerated tenderness, grabbed his battered satchel, and shuffled out the door. "Bye Mummy," he said with a loving smile to his smiling wife.

He then slammed the door before walking onto the pavement towards the train station. The house exhaled in his wake.

The train carriage was packed to suffocation point – a rolling coffin of polyester suits, greasy newspaper readers, and the occasional commuter whose deodorant had long since surrendered the fight.

Ian leaned against a pole, crisps in one hand, phone in the other. He thumbed out a text to Alison.

IAN: *Fancy lunch?*

The reply came back almost instantly, a cheerful little ping.

ALISON: *Love to!*

Ian smiled, a small, private thing, and shoved a handful of crisps into his mouth.

Alison was waiting in anticipation for Ian to arrive by the main office doors, clutching a big mug of tea, ready for him, in a red Post Office branded mug like a prize. The moment she spotted him, her face lit up.

"I made you tea," she said, holding it out like a gift.

Ian blinked, touched.

"Proper mug?"

"Big as your face," she said, laughing.

He took the cup, their fingers brushing briefly. They got into the lift together and ascended into their version of corporate hell.

Each of the six office floors at Post Office HQ had the oppressive atmosphere of a place designed by people who had never truly known joy. Grey cubicles stretched in every direction, forming a maze of dull partition walls pockmarked by old Blu Tack and motivational quotes printed in Comic Sans. The carpet was a muted, industrial grey, worn thin in the walkways and sticky in the corners, like no one had ever truly cleaned it – only rearranged the dirt.

Each cubicle was its own small island of quiet desperation: stacks of outdated folders, wilting succulents in novelty mugs, and departmental mugs that all read things like "I Survived GDPR Training 2019!" or "Ask Me About Parcel Pricing" in peeling gold letters. Mobile phones rang with the rhythm of mild regret, and the office printer let out the occasional shriek like it wanted to die but lacked the confidence.

Ian sat at one of his favourite desks on the second floor, a desk piled with unopened post, two half-crushed crisp packets, a ceramic mug that may once have been white, and a monitor that buzzed faintly in protest every time he moved the mouse. His keyboard was slightly sticky to the touch and had several keys with no visible lettering left.

He was typing rhythmically with one hand – slowly, with a single forefinger – while the other dipped in and out of a packet of dry roasted peanuts he was attacking with surgical dedication.

Beside him, Alison sat cross-legged on her ergonomic chair, sipping tea from a pink-and-black "World's Okayest Employee" mug. Her desk was neater, her screen brighter. They worked companionably, occasionally trading comments and private smirks – nothing overt, but something simmered just below the surface. The kind of easy familiarity that was either harmless or about to become a work scandal.

Alison leaned in slightly. "You've got peanut salt in your eyebrow."

Ian blinked. "It's a look."

"Bold."

"Dangerous. Like a dry roasted Bond villain."

She laughed softly, then sipped her tea – and that's when the shadow appeared.

Ruth.

She loomed over the cubicle partition like a poorly disguised spectre of corporate HR. Short, chubby, dressed in sharp high-street tailoring and an expression like she permanently suspected everyone of something. Her hair was scraped back into a severe ponytail, and her heels were the only sound the office had learned to fear. "Feeling better?" she asked, eyes narrowing. Her tone was suspicious, too smooth – like she was auditioning for a documentary about workplace poisonings.

Ian spun in his chair too quickly, the seat squeaking like it wanted to confess to something. He turned to face her mid-mouthful of peanuts, cheeks puffed out like a panicked rodent caught shoplifting trail mix. "Yeff fank oo," he spluttered through a cloud of salt and crushed legumes – bits of nut flying everywhere!

Ruth's expression curdled on contact. She stared at him, then sighed in disgust – a full-body exhalation that suggested she was mentally scrubbing her hands with sanitiser just from looking at him.

"Ugh," she said simply, then turned on her heel and marched off, her ponytail slicing the air back and forth behind her like a metronome of disdain.

Ian wiped his mouth with the back of his hand, caught a peanut shard in his beard, and flicked it into the bin with surprising accuracy.

Alison stifled a laugh behind her mug. "She definitely likes you," she said, still smiling.

"Absolutely," Ian nodded. "Nothing says erotic tension like wanting someone dead."

A moment passed. Alison set her mug down and tilted her head. "Fancy an early lunch?"

Ian pretended to think, still brushing salt off his jumper. "Italian?"

"End of the road?" asked Alison.

"You read my mind," said Ian agreeably.

Alison stood up slowly, smoothing down her skirt with easy grace. "You're sure you're not going to try to seduce me over pasta?"

"No promises," Ian said, grabbing his grubby coat. "But if I do, at least they do a decent tiramisu, which should make it worthwhile."

The walk to the restaurant was easy, natural. They fell into step without thinking. "So," Ian said, adjusting his bag, "how are the kids?"

"Brilliant," Alison said warmly. "Love being a mum. Even the chaos."

"And your husband?"

A cloud passed over Alison's face. "Always away. Never talks. Might as well have married a suitcase."

Ian nodded sympathetically, resisting the urge to say something glib.

Some silences weren't meant to be filled.

Trattoria Nunziata was tucked up a cobbled side street full of trendy jewellery and card shops close to Post Office HQ. It was the sort of place that didn't advertise because it didn't need to. The sign above the door was cracked ceramic tile, hand-painted in fading blue and terracotta. The windows were fogged with steam from decades of lunchtime service, and the smell – that glorious, all-consuming smell – wrapped itself around you the moment you stepped inside. It smelled like garlic and tomato and flour, and something faintly charred in a good way. Like someone's Nonna had weaponised comfort food.

Inside, the lighting was yellow and a bit too dim, the walls plastered with fading black-and-white photographs of serious men holding fish. The furniture didn't match. The tablecloths had seen better decades, and the menus were laminated and slightly sticky in a way that suggested love, not neglect.

The waiter, whose name might have been Enzo or Marco or possibly just "hey, boss," didn't so much take orders as argue you into the right decision.

By the time the plates hit the table, Ian was already two pint glasses of Negroni in. The table looked like it had been hit by a well-fed tornado.

There were olives in a chipped ceramic bowl, half-torn focaccia soaked in olive oil, a plate of lasagne that bled bechamel onto a napkin, crispy calamari rings with a scorched lemon wedge, and a rogue tiramisu Ian swore he hadn't ordered but had nearly inhaled anyway.

"Someone must've sent it over," he said with suspicious innocence, spoon deep in mascarpone. "Maybe it's from Ruth. She's always trying to get into my trousers."

Alison rolled her eyes and ordered Ian another drink with the subtle grace of a woman used to babysitting dangerous men.

Ian raised his pint glass – filled with a third Negroni – in mock salute.

"To overcompensating," he said grandly. They clinked glasses. Hers was a sensible small glass of white wine. Of course.

"Cheers," she said softly.

For a moment, they sat in the hum of the restaurant – forks clinking, conversations rising and falling around them in Italian, Cockney, mockney and everything in between. The kind of white noise that made you feel anonymous and safe.

Alison set her glass down and glanced up through her lashes. Her voice was light, playful. "You know I fancy you, don't you?"

Ian choked, the Negroni going down the wrong way in an instant rush of bitter citrus and panic. He coughed hard into his napkin, eyes watering, and looked at her through the haze of a near-death experience. "I'm old enough to be your dad," he rasped.

"That helps," she said, smiling with just the right amount of mischief. "Some of us girls have Daddy issues."

He laughed – or tried to – but there was something unsteady about it now. His heart had picked up pace and his face felt warm, and not just from the Negroni. Ian wiped his mouth and gestured at himself, vaguely defeated. "Look at me," he said. "I'm old. Smelly. Burpy. My socks are more air than fabric. I'm fairly sure I have food on my back somehow."

Alison shrugged like none of that mattered – or like it was the point. "I have funny little fantasies about you," she said, voice still soft, but her eyes never leaving his. "Very dark desires. You wouldn't believe some of the things I'd like to do to you!"

Ian blinked. "That's probably a GDPR breach," he muttered.

They both laughed then – real, relaxed, full-bodied – and something between them softened. Just enough.

Outside, the street traffic rumbled past. Inside, the plates shifted, and the second plate of tiramisu began to vanish in large spoonfuls again.

For a little while, the espionage and the blood and the body-count slipped quietly out the back door – and all that remained was a strange, scruffy man and the pretty young woman who maybe, just maybe, saw something beneath all the gravy stains.

Once Ian had paid the bill they strolled back to the office slowly, reluctant to end the moment. At one point, Alison reached for his hand, fingers brushing his. Ian swatted her away gently, chuckling. "Naughty," he said.

She laughed, a little breathless.

At the next corner, Ian veered off. "Right. Back to the grindstone. You'll manage without me?"

"Only just," Alison said, watching him disappear in the direction of the City.

He headed directly to his penthouse deep in the City. The penthouse was quiet, humming faintly with the scent of fine Scotch and leather. Ian checked his encrypted phone. A new text awaited:

*COVER STORY: Gym owner confirmed as prolific seducer of local housewives. No intel links. In hospital recovering. Clean wound. No infection.*

*Police think attacker – possibly a serial killer – took genitalia as a trophy."* Ian laughed.

He replied: "They're barking up the wrong tree with that." Ian sighed. He poured himself a whisky, slumping into his favourite chair. As he did so, his personal phone buzzed with a message.

ALISON: Thanks for lunch 😊 Let's do dinner soon. My treat this time x

Ian stared at the message for a long moment. Then deleted it without replying.

Before long Ian left his penthouse and made for the train station. The train rattled through the tunnels like an asthmatic dragon as Ian slumped into a seat, munching greasy crisps, and swigging whisky from a battered flask. On his lap: a flat cap, upturned. A passing man mistook the tableau for street theatre and tossed some change into the cap. Ian watched the coins land with a soft clink.

"Cheers, mate," he muttered, stuffing another crisp into his mouth. He made his way home and was glad to be able to spend some time with Susan. To try to understand what had tempted her to very nearly play away with the philandering gym trainer.

The house was warm. Familiar. Smelling faintly of fabric softener, last night's stew, and the kind of vanilla-scented candle that Susan always bought on offer and lit halfway down, then forgot about.

Ian shut the front door behind him with a soft click and stood there for a second in the quiet. His coat still smelled of chip shop vinegar and cold train carriage, but the hallway smelled of home – faintly damp, faintly clean, faintly dog. The carpet was that tough, beige stuff designed to survive decades of feet and spills, and on the wall hung a faded framed poster from a long-forgotten National Trust day out, slightly crooked.

The sitting room glowed with low yellow lamplight and the flicker of the television. Susan was curled on the sofa in her usual spot – feet tucked beneath her, reading a paperback whose creased spine suggested it had been passed around three book clubs and left in a holiday let before she got hold of it. She wore a thick cardigan over a pair of joggers with a mystery stain on one knee and a slogan t-shirt that read "World's Best Mum (According to Max, 2014)".

Her hair was swept into a casual knot, her reading glasses perched low on her nose, and a half-drunk mug of Earl Grey sat balanced precariously on the armrest beside her. A half-knitted scarf spilled from a basket on the floor. An advert for life insurance burbled gently in the background.

Ian paused in the doorway for a moment, just watching. There was something strangely cinematic about it – not in a grand way, but in that quiet, low-stakes sense of someone who had arrived safely at the last station on the line. It was domesticity in its purest, undiluted form.

"Good day, Daddy?" Susan asked, not looking up from her book. Her voice was absent minded, familiar, laced with the comfort of a hundred evenings exactly like this one.

"Always is when you're at the end of it," Ian said softly. He crossed the room and dropped down beside her with the kind of weight that made the entire sofa sigh in protest. The cushions shifted like tectonic plates under his bulk, and Susan tilted gently sideways, letting her head rest against his arm without comment.

Susan Taylor had always been a woman of curated contradictions. On the one hand: She wore a worn Cartier watch, given to her by Ian for her 40th birthday – not because she needed it, but because she liked the way it didn't really keep perfect time. On the other: she kept three amethysts and a petrified fossilised walnut in her handbag at all times, because a woman in Totnes once told her they were good for balance. She could talk fluently about chakras, shadow work, or the energy vortex of Trent Park, but also knew how to make gravy with her eyes closed and had once reversed a Volvo estate through a narrow Cornish lane with brutal, terrifying precision at 45 miles an hour. At heart, she was an Earth Mother in a cashmere wrap. Slightly mystical, deeply practical, and always ready to politely destroy someone in at Parent-Teacher Association meeting if they used the word "less" when they meant "fewer."

She and Ian had met at Durham University in the 1980s, when they'd both joined the student Communist Party society, mostly out of idealism and for a free helping of the lentil stew that was always on offer. She'd been sharp, brilliant, confident. Ian had been covered in biro and thought Trotsky was a kind of cheese.

She'd loved him anyway. Or at least, she'd loved the way he could make her laugh until she had snorted loudly in the Marxist reading group at an inappropriate moment. They'd grown up, left the party behind, and replaced the revolution with a mortgage and a large dog that farted like a foghorn.

These days though, she carried a quiet sense of disappointment around the house like a scented candle. She called Ian 'Daddy', but never quite stopped sounding like she might one day phone the council and have him collected as an abandoned appliance.

Still, she was loyal. Fiercely so. Beneath the sarcasm and sighs and herbal tea, there was steel.

She didn't quite know exactly what Ian was – but she knew, on some level, that he was more than he looked on the surface.

In the living room, Tolstoy flumped down at their feet with a theatrical grunt, curling his massive body into the rug like a particularly judgmental hearth rug. His tail thumped once, then went still.

Ian exhaled heavily, scratched his belly through his jumper, and let out a slow, bubbling burp that echoed faintly off the mantelpiece. Tolstoy responded with a deep, rumbling fart that rolled out across the room like mustard gas.

Susan waved a hand in front of her face, grimacing theatrically. "You'll never change," she said, laughing.

"Let's hope not," Ian replied, grinning – though he opened the window an inch out of mercy.

The television played on – now some home renovation show, where a couple in matching gilets were arguing about whether or not to knock through a load-bearing wall. The radiator ticked as it cooled. Somewhere in the kitchen, the boiler hummed like an old friend.

Outside, the wind rattled the windows in their frames.

But inside, in this small, ageing house full of socks with holes and mugs with chipped rims, the world had stopped spinning. And for once – beautifully, improbably – everything was still.

## Chapter Five
# The Toast of Tehran

*"Avoid attachments. Or at least, make sure they're not fluent in Russian."*
**~ Foreign Asset Risk Guidelines**

## Chapter 5

# The Toast of Tehran

Ian Taylor had a complex relationship with ambition. He wasn't against it, exactly – he just believed most ambitions were poorly thought out. Buying a bigger house you couldn't afford. Running marathons with dodgy knees. Climbing career ladders that led nowhere but another bloody cubicle. But poisoning a man without anyone noticing? That was an ambition Ian understood and respected. And today, he had work to do.

He sat hunched over his desk at Post Office HQ, a figure of shambolic desolation. The pot noodle on the corner of his desk had given up pretending to be edible an hour ago. Beside it, a mug filled with a suspicious amber liquid. Officially it was cold tea. Unofficially, Ian was three fingers deep into a bottle of Highland Park 18-Year-Old.

He typed with one finger, slowly, deliberately, hammering out yet another thrilling missive about customer mailings and data compliance. From a distance, he looked exactly how he wanted to look: Defeated. Hopeless. Forgettable. Which made it all the more jarring when Alison swanned up to his desk, dressed to kill. Her lipstick was a little bolder than usual, her heels a little higher. She leaned in, close enough for him to catch a whiff of her expensive perfume.

"Ian," she said, her voice warm and bright. "Any chance you're free tonight for dinner?" She perched on the edge of his desk, her hand brushing his leg – a casual accident that wasn't casual at all. "I know a rooftop bar that serves an amazing steak tartare and negronis," she added, voice dipping to a playful murmur.

Ian smiled faintly. "Can't tonight," he said. "Got plans."

Alison pouted — beautifully, skillfully. "You're dodging me. Admit it."

Ian leaned back, tapping a biro against his chin, enjoying the game more than he should. "Maybe I'm just hard to catch," he said, voice pitched low.

Alison laughed, tossing her hair over her shoulder.

Ian watched her go, heart ticking a little faster. *Maybe she actually fancied him,* he thought,

By three o'clock, Ian was out of the building. He cut through the city's streets like a ghost: weaving through suits and shoppers, past grim-faced cycle couriers and bored taxi drivers. He checked over his shoulder twice. No tail. Good. He slipped into a side alley, tugged his jacket tighter, and disappeared.

When he emerged on the next street over, something in his walk had changed – a new tension, a new sharpness, coiled and lethal. The mask was slipping. The real Ian Taylor was coming up for air.

The lift opened directly into his penthouse, its whisper-quiet doors parting like curtains before a one-man performance. The space greeted Ian like an old accomplice not with warmth, but with a familiar, curated silence. The air was cool and still, the lighting dimmed just enough to soften the edges of danger. It smelled faintly of cedar and clean leather – a scent designed to evoke discretion, wealth, and restraint. The only sound was the low hum of concealed ventilation and the distant pulse of London beneath glass.

He stepped inside and closed the door behind him. With the same unhurried, almost reverent precision he reserved for weapon prep, Ian peeled off his Post Office skin. The polyester shirt – streaked with biro ink and a stubborn soup stain – was unbuttoned with mechanical indifference and dropped in a heap beside the door. The trousers followed, limp and crumpled – the deflated remains of another life. His socks, mismatched and riddled with holes, were peeled away and left wherever they landed. Naked, he crossed the warm wooden floor, padding toward the enormous shower room with the solid grace of a man who'd done this hundreds of times before. Tolstoy, if present, would have known not to follow.

Inside, the wet room hissed to life with a button press. Water gushed from a rainfall head in perfect symmetry – not hot, not cold. Precisely calibrated. Ian stepped under the torrent and stood there, letting the day dissolve off him: the smell of burnt pot noodles, the lingering trace of train-seat sweat, the faint clinging regret of domestic normality. He scrubbed, thoroughly. Face. Hands. Neck. Behind the ears.

Beneath the nails. By the time he emerged, towelling himself dry with luxury Egyptian cotton, Ian Taylor had disappeared. In his place stood someone sharper. Someone formidable.

Dressed in a tailored black Armani suit – the sort you didn't buy off the peg unless you were a fool with money. Ian looked taller, cleaner, harder. The jacket fitted perfectly across the shoulders, tapering into a subtle V at the waist. The trousers broke just above gleaming black shoes shined to an uncompromising mirror polish. His crisp white shirt was fresh from the press, collar stiff enough to slice paper. Cufflinks: matte gunmetal. Understated. Expensive. Lethal, if required. On his wrist, a Rolex Daytona Panda gleamed, black sub-dials, white main dial, stainless steel casing, the kind of timepiece that whispered wealth in 15 different languages without ever raising its voice. His hair, still damp from the shower, was slicked back with some light pomade, just enough to suggest control without vanity. He radiated confidence – not the blustering kind, but the quiet, heatless kind you can't fake. The kind that got people killed in distant cities.

He moved to the large mirror and pressed the button that opened up his mini armoury. It clicked open, revealing an array of formidable weaponry. He selected his work tools with care, each item nested in a custom-cut compartment like surgical instruments: Twin spring-loaded daggers disguised as black Montblanc pens. Two compact silenced pistols, lightweight enough for discretion, heavy enough for consequence. A small vial of colourless powder, sealed inside a shockproof glass cylinder, cushioned in velvet. It looked like nothing. But it was something very final.

Each piece was tested, checked, and then concealed – in hidden jacket linings, in specially designed pockets sewn into the inner waistband of the trousers, in a pocket sewn behind the lapel that no tailor would ever admit to.

He stood in front of the full-length mirror. No lint. No creases. No excess. Everything where it needed to be.

He adjusted the collar, checked the pistol weight once, and nodded once – not at his reflection, but at the man underneath it. "Showtime," he said under his breath. And then the lift doors opened again, and Ian Taylor walked into the night – not as a Post Office marketing manager, or a henpecked husband, or a man who smelled faintly of biscuits – but as something else entirely.

He jumped in a black cab and asked the driver to take him to The Radisson Hotel.

The Radisson on Westminster Bridge sat brooding over the city like an old colonial general – all polished marble, looming columns, and understated threat.

On the pavement outside:

Two businessmen smoke expensive cigars.

A pair of tourists argue over a map.

A beggar nurses a cup of cold coffee, invisible to everyone else.

Ian slipped around the side of the building, blending into the service entrance crowd: staff in black waistcoats, harassed event organisers clutching clipboards, delivery drivers shouting into mobile phones. Inside, the air smelled of polish, anxiety, and money. A manager with slicked-back hair intercepted him. "Are you the one from London Events Group?" the man asked, distracted.

Ian smiled warmly. "That's right," he said. "Special event concierge."

The manager barely glanced at his ID badge – a beautifully forged piece of nothingness – before ushering him inside. "OK. We'll get you set up," the manager muttered.

Ian made his way to the Ballroom. The ballroom was obscene in the way only high-end diplomacy could be – a monument to corporate vanity lacquered in old money and blind indulgence. Crystal chandeliers, each the size of a compact car and shaped like frozen explosions, hung from the gilded ceiling like they were trying to outshine one another. The light they cast was soft but unrelenting – the sort of glow that smoothed over wrinkles and cast flattering shadows, while still exposing every under-polished shoe and nervous bead of sweat. The walls were dressed in cream and gold damask, interrupted only by enormous mirrors and tastefully mounted oil paintings of 18th-century nobility who looked faintly ashamed to be involved. Up-lighting cast soft amber washes across marble columns that served no structural purpose but had each apparently cost more than a starter home in Islington. Endless rows of round tables, each draped in pristine white linen and burdened with centrepieces of blood-red roses and polished silver, groaned under the weight of absurd appetisers: carved towers of smoked salmon, tumbling nests of Beluga caviar, miniature beef Wellingtons aligned with military precision.

A gloved army of waiters scurried through the space like anxious ants, ferrying flutes of vintage Cristal across the room, trays of foie gras on brioche circling in a tight ballet around diplomats, minor royals, oil magnates, and political donors with suspiciously perfect teeth. The air smelled of truffles and expensive perfume and something just faintly sour beneath it all – like fear, or anticipation.

And through it all, Ian Taylor moved like he belonged. He wore his outfit well – black waistcoat, white gloves, a pressed collar stiff enough to decapitate someone at speed. A small silver pin on his lapel read EVENTS GROUP, the fabricated identity checked and re-checked against the hotel's guest list and security protocols. It was all legitimate – right down to the signature on his timesheet. In his left hand, he balanced a silver tray loaded with champagne flutes, his movements fluid and effortless. He didn't walk – he glided, weaving between clusters of conversation with a casual grace that didn't draw attention but didn't defer, either.

He swept past an Emirati oil minister in a silk keffiyeh. Nodded politely to the French Ambassador and his botoxed wife. Stepped aside for a heavily armed security detail flanking a tech billionaire who smelled of saffron and self-importance.

Ian was invisible. But in control.

His tray dipped slightly, and in one smooth, shameless motion, he plucked a big handful of truffle nuts from the centrepiece on Table Nine – a pyramid of pecan, pistachio and black truffle-dusted almonds – and shoved them into his mouth behind the shelter of a napkin. He chewed, eyes narrowing slightly with pleasure. They were absurdly good. *How the other half live,* he thought. From a side table where drinks were being replenished, he snagged a half-finished glass of vintage Armagnac – abandoned, still cold, still golden – and downed it in one quiet, glorious gulp. It was like a fine syrup exploding in his mouth. He grinned to himself, licking the corner of his mouth as he moved on. *Assassin's perks,* he joked to himself!

Somewhere in the crowd, someone would soon die. Probably quietly. Probably quickly. Possibly painfully. But for now, Ian just kept moving – remaining invisible.

There. He had spotted him. The Iranian.

He was exactly as the dossier had described – and yet seeming somehow more dangerous in the flesh. Tall. Composed. Silver hair slicked back with surgical precision, not a strand out of place. His navy-blue suit was flawlessly tailored, the sort of cut that whispered military past and diplomatic immunity in the same breath. The lapels were narrow, the shoulders just sharp enough to suggest discipline, and the pocket square was folded with the kind of geometry you didn't get from a haberdashery – you got it from training.

He stood near the centre of the ballroom, a swirl of minor diplomats and bloated consultants orbiting around him like obedient satellites. His posture was effortless, his expression pleasant, his smile faint – almost apologetic – but it never once reached his eyes. Those remained flat and cold – almost dead. The eyes of a man who had authorised things, not with anger, but necessity.

Ian adjusted course, veering just a fraction to the right – enough to bring him within reach without drawing attention. He pretended to offer a flute of champagne to a group of laughing guests nearby, his white-gloved hand steady as stone. The tray dipped slightly as he passed the target. Polished silver, gleaming glass. All eyes elsewhere.

His hand moved fast – quick enough to be unnoticeable, slow enough not to break rhythm. He performed the switch smoothly: the Iranian's original glass – untouched, sweating faintly – slid onto the tray, and a nearly identical flute slid into its place. Inside: the colourless powder, perfectly dissolved. Tasteless. Scentless. Invisible. Deadly. No fuss. No fanfare. Just a servant doing his job. Perfect.

The Iranian reached for the fresh glass, fingers brushing the stem, but just as it reached his lips, another man descended upon him like a thunderclap of inappropriate volume and colonial aftershave. "Ali!" the newcomer boomed – thick Northern accent, ruddy cheeks, stocky frame wrapped in an ill-fitting tux that had clearly been hired with little enthusiasm and less time. His hand clapped down hard on the Iranian's shoulder with the overconfidence of someone who'd once closed a deal over golf in Dubai and never quite recovered.

The Iranian turned, startled, eyebrows twitching upward in controlled annoyance. The glass – the poisoned glass – wobbled in his hand.

Ian acted without thinking. He shifted one step closer and brought his foot down sharply – heel first – onto the newcomer's shoe. Hard.

"OW! What the –?!" the man yelped, recoiling, hopping on one foot like a startled terrier. The glass slipped from the Iranian's hand in that slow-motion way only adrenaline could produce. It tumbled forward, tilting toward the floor, its perfect amber contents about to be lost in a £300-a-plate puddle.

Ian caught it mid-air, fingers closing around the stem with surgical precision. His face didn't change. His body didn't flinch. He simply caught it and turned the motion into a polished handoff, returning it to the Iranian with the soft, blank efficiency of a man who had spent his entire adult life making sure rich people didn't embarrass themselves. "Careful, sir," Ian said, his voice smooth, clipped, anonymous. "This one's particularly good."

The Iranian let out a soft chuckle, the moment of interruption already dismissed. "Thanks," he said – and then downed the drink in one clean, confident swallow, as if to emphasise the point.

Ian offered a faint bow, just enough to be deferential, and took the now-empty glass back onto his tray, tucking it toward the back, hidden among the others. He turned and moved off, not too quickly, not too slow. No one noticed him leave. He slid between the guests like smoke, like a shadow, like he'd never been there at all. A ghost.

Once he had found a table to park the tray of empty glasses – except one – Ian strode into the nearest alleyway, smashed the glass against the pavement, and swept the fragments into a storm drain. Evidence gone. Mission complete. Time to scarper into the night.

\*\*\*

It started with a cough. Soft at first — no more than a polite throat-clear, the kind of thing you'd hear at any black-tie event where rich men drank cold champagne and talked over each other. Then another. Sharper this time. Wet at the end.

The Iranian shifted slightly on his feet, placing a hand on the back of a nearby chair, his posture tightening almost imperceptibly. His shoulders stiffened. He coughed again — this one a proper hack, deeper, like something was being wrenched loose inside his lungs. Guests began to glance over – a ripple of movement across a nearby table as people subtly leaned in or leaned away. The fourth cough was violent. Sudden. It bent him double and sent a fine mist of spittle across his polished dress shoes. Now people were standing, watching. The woman beside him – a sleek brunette in a red silk dress – let out a short, high shriek, her champagne flute tipping sideways onto the white tablecloth, bleeding gold into the fine white linen. Her chair scraped back with a screech.

"Is there a doctor?!" someone shouted – a man's voice, thick with urgency and just enough fear to silence a cluster of conversation nearby. The Iranian coughed again – long, convulsive, wracked with force. His face was red now, veins rising at his temple, one hand clawing weakly at his tie, the other fumbling for the back of another chair that collapsed under his weight as he fell forward onto the floor. There was a crash of shattering glass and a scream – high, breathless, genuine. Panic began to blossom like a forest fire. Several people surged forward. Others backed away. A waiter dropped an entire tray of Cristal that exploded on the marble floor like a shotgun blast. Chairs tipped. A man near the bar called for security, barking into a walkie-talkie like it might solve something. The Iranian rolled onto his back, eyes wide and sightless now, his mouth foaming, opening and closing without sound, like a fish stranded on carpet. The ballroom – that temple of wealth and control – had gone sideways in under thirty seconds. And Ian Taylor? Ian was already long gone.

By the time the first person began CPR and the defibrillator was on its way down from reception, Ian was already half a block up Vandon Street, walking at a pace that was just brisk enough not to seem hurried. His posture was relaxed. Casual. Intentional.

He peeled off his white gloves one finger at a time and was about to drop them into a wire bin outside a Pret a Manger sandwich shop, like they were till receipts – when he stopped. *No,* he thought, *mustn't leave any evidence.* He slipped the gloves deep into his jacket pocket. He would get Jim to destroy everything tomorrow. A faint trail of the finest Armagnac still lingered in the air behind him.

The sounds of the city were unchanged – buses whooshing past, cab tyres hissing in the damp, someone playing saxophone badly under an overpass – but Ian felt the shift behind him like a seismic echo. Somewhere back there, men were shouting. Phones were ringing. CCTV cameras were being checked. Blame was being passed around like a hot potato. But Ian didn't look back. He kept walking. Into the gathering dusk. Into the crowd. Into nothing. The air was thick with diesel fumes and fried onions – that unmistakable London scent, equal parts transport and late-night regret. Somewhere close, a kebab van hissed with overuse, its metal hood stained with the ghosts of three thousand drunken nights. Horns honked in the middle distance. A cyclist swore creatively as he weaved around a pedestrian holding a Pret bag like a weapon of mass destruction.

Ian moved fast but steady. He kept his head low, his jacket collar up, and his pace just under a jog. Fast enough to suggest purpose. Slow enough to avoid notice. The last of the city's rush-hour commuters still poured into Bank Station like ants escaping a burning log – blazers creased, expressions hollow, earbuds welded in. He blended in easily. To anyone watching, he was just another well-dressed man heading toward the Underground — maybe a broker late for dinner, or someone trying to impress an expensive mistress.

His hands were steady. His stride even. But his heart was still knocking out Morse code from the events in the hotel ballroom.

He was half a step from disappearing down the road in the direction of his penthouse when something caught the corner of his eye. A flicker of familiarity. He turned his head – just slightly – and then he saw her. It was Alison.

Leaning casually against a lamppost, one foot crossed over the other, scrolling her phone. She looked relaxed, amused by something on the screen. Her dark blazer was buttoned tight, her blouse tucked just-so. She looked every inch the charming, harmless coworker from the office – but now she was going to see him in his other persona – his smarter alto ego. She looked up. Their eyes met. Recognition struck them both like a match.

"Ian?!" she cried. Her face lit up. A smile broke across her lips – wide, warm, and just a little too sharp. "Wow. You look amazing. All dressed up!" she said, stepping away from the lamppost with the kind of easy confidence that made danger feel like flirtation. "Where have you been tonight?"

Ian's mind was racing. Every scenario, every cover story, every excuse – all of it fell apart under the pressure of her gaze. He had seconds. Maybe even less. His mouth opened before he could stop it. "Sorry," he blurted, in the worst thick Russian accent he could manage – a breathless mash of vowels and panic. "No English. Runnings for train. Sorrys. Dosvedanya"

He dipped his head, sidestepped – tried to move past, feet already angling for escape. But Alison didn't move. She just tilted her head slightly, eyes narrowing as if studying something under glass. And then – in perfect, fluent, native Russian, smooth as silk: "Oh! Apologies," she said, the language sliding off her tongue like it belonged there. "I thought you were someone I work with."

Ian stopped cold. He felt it before he understood it – a full-body jolt, like the air had thickened or gravity had shifted. A drop of cold sweat traced down the back of his neck beneath the crisp collar of his suit. His throat tightened. The corners of the world darkened just slightly, as if a spotlight had flicked on above him.

She was still smiling. Like nothing had happened. Like she hadn't just detonated a truth bomb in his lap.

Ian muttered something under his breath – something unprintable and definitely not in Russian – then turned on his heel and bolted. Gone.

Shoulders hunched, legs working fast, he slipped into the crowd like a stone dropped into a very deep fast-flowing river. Behind him, Alison stood still. The smile remained. But now, it was something else. Colder. Sharper. She was focussing and so was Ian.

Ian made his way to his penthouse rapidly; he needed to get off the streets as quickly as possible. He locked the door of the penthouse behind him with shaking hands. Poured himself three fingers of thirty-five-year-old Glenmorangie directly into a glass the size of his fist and knocked it back in a single huge gulp! He pulled out his encrypted phone.

IAN: *Just bumped into Alison from work. She spoke fluent Russian. Native level. I might have misjudged her. Can you check her out?*

The reply came back fast. *OK. We'll look into it.*

Ian sat heavily on the sofa, drinking 35-year-old whisky, now straight from the bottle. The city glowed below. Danger lurked closer than he'd realised. He felt so stupid. He had seriously underestimated Alison.

It was time to change back into his home clothes and to get back home. He dropped all of his clothing, including the white gloves he's been wearing, into a black back and sealed it. Jim and other MI5 cleaners would swing by later to take everything away that linked Ian to tonight's events and destroy them.

Ian had another shower, then made himself grubby looking and climbed back into his day clothes. A black Prius rolled up to the corner outside of his penthouse like any other late-night Uber: slightly too quiet, slightly too late, and with the faint smell of Febreze trying to cover something deeper. Ian clocked the car before it pulled to a stop. He always did.

The rear window eased down an inch, revealing a bushy brown moustache – the kind that looked like it had been glued on in the back of a moving van – and a pair of thick NHS-issue glasses that refracted the dashboard lights into strange shapes. "Evening," said the Uber driver, cheerfully. His voice was unmistakable. It was Jim. "Hop in. I hear you've had a busy night. It's all over the news."

Ian climbed into the back, settling into the cracked leather seat with a grunt. "You could say that" he muttered, undoing his jacket button and exhaling deeply. "Somebody poisoned my liver with truffle nuts and now it wants a divorce."

Jim glanced at him in the rear-view mirror, moustache twitching slightly as he grinned. "Well, that's high society for you. Posh snacks. Terrible hospitality."

They pulled off quietly, merging with the slow pulse of evening traffic drifting north. Outside, London blurred past – the statues and townhouses giving way to kebab shops, shuttered corner stores, and the odd glowing vape café that hadn't existed six months ago. They passed through Camden, the streets quieter now, but not asleep – tattooed men smoking outside music venues, women in glittery dresses waiting for night buses, teenagers on scooters chasing nothing in particular. Neon spilled onto the pavement from the window of a Caribbean chicken shop. A fox trotted past a skip. Somewhere, someone was playing a saxophone badly but confidently.

By the time they reached Kentish Town, the city had shed its gloss completely. The shopfronts were old, tired. Laundrettes and betting shops. A post office with bars on the windows. The air smelled of exhaust, old chip fat, spilt cider and tramps bedding down for the night.

"Want to pick up some fish and chips on the way home?" Jim asked casually, tapping the steering wheel in rhythm with the indicator.

"God, yes," Ian sighed, suddenly aware of the gnawing hollow in his gut. "Those canapé things wouldn't feed a mouse. More foam than food. One of them was just a thing like a pea on a cracker. A single bloody pea."

"London dining at its finest," Jim said, indicating right.

They pulled up outside a big family-run Greek Cypriot fish and chip shop at the corner of a junction where four different roads met. 'Poseidon's Catch' was painted in bold blue letters across the top, the windows steamed up and glowing with harsh fluorescent light. It smelled divine. The kind of place where everything – fish, chips, battered sausage, even some of their kebabs, chicken portions, onion rings, pickled eggs, Mars Bars – were cooked in the same fryer and all the better for it.

Inside, behind the misted counter, stood Nikos, the eternally cheerful owner with forearms like ham shanks and the grin of a man who truly believed in fried food as a healthy option. "Ian!" Nikos beamed, pointing a pair of tongs like a greeting. "You come late tonight, my friend! Long day?"

"You could say that," Ian nodded, scanning the overhead menu like it was written in code.

"You want the usual?"

Ian thought for a moment, then nodded. "Make it massive."

"How massive?" Nikos asked, arching a thick eyebrow.

"Biblically massive."

Nikos laughed and got to work. Ten minutes later, Ian emerged clutching a greasy paper-wrapped parcel the size of a briefcase, already bleeding vinegar through the bottom. The heat soaked through his coat. The smell hit like a nostalgic uppercut.

Back in the car, he tore the parcel open like a wolf with a lamb.

By the time they turned off onto Ian's street, he'd eaten half the chips, almost all of the battered cod, and was eyeing the kebab meat as if it had personally wronged him.

Jim slowed at the top of the road.

"I'll walk it from here," Ian said, licking a fleck of ketchup off his thumb. "Give the neighbours a break. Don't want them thinking I've gone all glamorous – with a private driver and whatnot."

Jim snorted. "Yeah. Wouldn't want to ruin your image."

Ian climbed out, clutching the warm, half-empty bundle to his chest like a sacred object. The night was quiet now. Residential. Curtains drawn. TVs flickering behind net curtains. A fox picked at a bin bag halfway down the road. The ordinary world. He breathed in. Home. And walked on.

Grease-stained paper parcel clutched in one hand like a sacred offering; Ian strolled down his street with the contentment of a man whose dinner had been freshly fried and wrapped in newspaper. The remaining cod – still steaming, its golden batter cracking with every bite – vanished steadily as he wandered past the manicured front gardens of his neighbours. He ate with unseemly joy, stuffing mouthfuls of chips into his face like a man who hadn't committed a high-profile political assassination just ninety minutes earlier.

His fingers shone with fat and cooking oil. Salt clung to the stubble on his chin, along with all sorts of other remnants of snacks and food. A blob of ketchup slid down his sleeve and was wiped clean with the inside of his jacket. He didn't slow down. He didn't care.

Many of the houses along the street were nearly identical – a parade of polite brickwork and frosted windows, each one trying to out-cottage the next. Edwardian semis with highly polished brass knockers. Pebble-dashed dreams with solar-powered fairy lights and bay trees in matching ceramic pots. Not a curtain out of place, not a hedge untamed. One house had a tiny white picket fence and a ceramic duck wearing a seasonal scarf. Another boasted a motion-sensor security light that pinged on as Ian passed, casting him in the harsh glow usually reserved for burglars and Deliveroo drivers. Ian offered the light a middle finger and kept walking.

His breath steamed in the cool air. Somewhere in the distance, a dog barked once. A light went out in an upstairs bedroom window as he approached – probably someone who'd spotted him coming and decided not to chance Ian seeing him.

He passed the grey house with the hydrangeas shaped like lollipops. The redbrick with the constantly weeded driveway. And then: Mr Duffy's house. Perfect. Unnervingly so. The hedge was freshly clipped into an unnaturally straight line, like it had been shaved with a laser. Not a leaf out of place. The windows gleamed. Even the front path had been pressure-washed into submission.

Ian paused briefly. Looked at the balled-up fish and chip paper (now empty) in his hand – greasy, limp, reeking of salt and vinegar. Then, without ceremony, he jammed it deep into the heart of Mr Duffy's hedge. A small act of rebellion. Or maybe just littering. Hard to tell.

He wiped his fingers on the inside of his coat and carried on towards his home. As he reached his own front gate – paint flaking, latch slightly bent – the porch light flicked on automatically, throwing a warm yellow glow across the cracked paving slabs and lopsided flowerpot he kept meaning to sort out. And then as he opened the front door with a click: a blur of movement and a crash into the opening door.

Tolstoy. The giant Russian Black Terrier launched himself at the door like a canine freight train, tongue lolling, tail wagging in huge, swooshing arcs. Ian opened the door, and the dog barrelled into him, howling, rearing up, front paws thudding against his chest. "All right, boy," Ian laughed, staggering slightly under the weight. "Save it for the burglars and the KGB extraction teams."

Tolstoy dropped back onto all fours and circled Ian once before trotting outside and then back up the front steps with the self-importance of a dog who knew he outranked the postman, the cat next door, and most of the family.

Ian closed the door after them both and walked towards the living room. The warmth hit him immediately – the smell of old central heating, something vaguely floral from one of Susan's plug-ins, and a trace of laundry powder.

Behind him, Tolstoy licked Ian's hands more in search of cod and grease than due to love and then collapsed in the hallway with a grunt.

Ian paused. Took one last deep breath. Home. Sanity. Chaos. He grinned.

The house was dimly lit, quiet in that particular way homes get when most of the world is asleep and the radiators have just started to cool. But Susan was still up. She was curled in the corner of the sofa, legs tucked under a crocheted blanket, a battered paperback splayed open across her lap. The spine was cracked and the pages dog-eared — something light, probably romantic, but with just enough mystery to keep her turning pages. A cup of tea, now half-cold, sat untouched on the side table next to a lavender-scented candle she'd forgotten to blow out.

She looked up as Ian closed the door behind him, her expression softening instantly. Her eyes said *you're late,* but her smile said *thank God you're home.*

Ian peeled off his coat and wandered into the living room with the loose-limbed gait of a man who had eaten too much and killed too many people that day. He dropped down beside her with a theatrical sigh, the sofa wheezing under the sudden redistribution of weight. "Couldn't you sleep, Mummy?" he asked, loosening his belt a notch and tugging at the waistband of his trousers like they were personally to blame for the evening's excesses.

"Hi, Daddy," Susan said gently, her voice low and a little scratchy from disuse. "I'm glad you're home. Long day?"

"You could say that." He yawned. "Big event. Elbows flying. Bit of a champagne riot."

"Have you eaten?"

Ian hesitated. "Had something small, some nibbles," he lied, wiping a smear of vinegar from the corner of his mouth. "But I'm sure I could manage a bit more if you've cooked something..."

Susan smiled – that small, knowing, long-married smile – and she quickly disappeared into the kitchen without a word, slippers whispering across the lino.

Five minutes later, she returned with two plates of pie and mash. The good stuff – homemade. The pie crust cracked golden, oozing rich brown gravy. The mash whipped smooth just right, a swirl in the middle for the gravy to pool into. She handed him a plate and settled beside him again. They ate in companionable silence. Not the strained silence of people with things to say and no courage to say them – but the tired, settled quiet of two people who'd already said everything that mattered. They ate like old soldiers after a long campaign.

Ian forked pie into his mouth in slow, reverent bites, gravy already trailing down his chin and into his beard like a veteran hiker falling into a familiar valley. He didn't care. The heat, the starch, the salt – it grounded him. Pulled him away from memories of the ballroom. From the eyes that didn't smile. From the choking diplomat and the shattered glass.

Across the room, the television flickered soundlessly. A looping news banner crawled across the bottom of the screen.

*BREAKING:* Iranian Diplomat Dies at London Gala – US Intelligence involvement suspected.

Susan's eyes drifted up to the TV just as she reached for her cup of tea. Her gaze lingered for a second longer than it should have.

Ian didn't look. He knew what was on the screen. He focused on cutting the last corner of his pie.

But Susan's gaze didn't return to her book. Instead, it slid to his wrist – and stopped. "Ian! Where on earth did you get that Rolex from?" Her voice wasn't sharp. But it had that edge – the same one she used when she spotted suspicious online purchases or extra empty whisky bottles in the recycling bin. Ian froze. Just slightly. Just enough for her to notice. "Erm..." he started, and it came out too fast. "It's a snide. You know a fake. Pete at work lent it to me. For the do tonight. I didn't want to go in with my old Casio – the strap's a bit buggered."

Susan tilted her head. Just a fraction. "You don't usually care about appearances, Daddy." Her tone was soft, almost amused. But her eyes were still on the watch, eying it suspiciously.

Ian, gravy pooling at the corner of his plate, crumbs in his beard, gave her his most earnest, wide-eyed grin. He even reached for a napkin and dabbed at his chin in an attempt at dignity. "I like to look smart when I'm out representing the Post Office," he said. "Dignity and all that."

She didn't answer. She just looked doubtful. Just looked at him for a long, quiet moment – as if she were holding the watch and the mashed potato and the strange hours and the distance between them all at once – and trying to see the shape they made when assembled.

Eventually, she picked up her fork again and gave a tiny shrug. "Well," she murmured. "As long as it's just on loan."

Ian exhaled – slowly – and attacked the last of his mash like it owed him money. Across the room, Tolstoy was now sprawled in front of the radiator, legs in the air, paws twitching faintly in a dream chase. He snorted once, then let rip a deep, vibratory fart that echoed off the floorboards.

Susan wrinkled her nose and waved a hand.

Ian burped in sympathy and took a sip of the tea Susan had made for him – lukewarm now, but comforting.

Life, in all its messy, mashed glory, marched on.

Chapter Six
# A Clean Break

*"You're never off duty. Especially in suburbia."*
**~ Domestic Surveillance Training Slides, Slide 7 of 314**

## Chapter 6

# A Clean Break

Some mornings whispered promises of peace. Others rumbled the coming of war. Ian Taylor woke up to the gentle hum of his secure phone vibrating against the nightstand. Susan was still asleep. He blinked blearily at the screen, scrolling through numbers that made most people's annual salaries look like rounding errors:

£26 million in an offshore account.

£12 million in Bitcoin and Ethereum.

£49 million across global shares and bonds.

And the money for last night's hit had already cleared into his current bank account – a cool £3 million – topping that account up to over £7 million.

He grinned, scratching his belly through the threadbare fabric of his grubby Y-fronts. The elastic had long given up hope, but Ian, stubborn as ever, refused to upgrade. He shuffled toward the bathroom, farting with each step like a deranged bagpipe.

When he eventually came downstairs, from a very long session sitting on the loo, the kitchen smelled better than it had any right to: bacon, eggs, buttered toast, grilled tomatoes – a full English Breakfast laid out with suspicious neatness.

Susan hovered by the counter, humming softly to herself. Ian froze, instantly suspicious.

"Morning, Daddy," she said brightly. "Made your favourite."

Ian scratched the back of his neck, wary.

"You feeling alright?"

Susan smiled, almost shyly. "Just being nice. It's not illegal...yet."

Max, already hunched over a bowl of cereal, looked up with a smirk. "Jeez, you two are like lovesick teenagers these days. What happened to constantly mocking Dad?"

Ian and Susan grinned at each other, giggling. Without a word, Ian wrapped his arms around her, burying his face in her hair. She laughed, thumping his chest gently.

Max gagged audibly.

At that moment, Daisy slouched into the room, clutching a plate piled high with smashed avocado and toast. "For God's sake," she said, horrified. "Get a room."

"We have a room," Ian said, winking at Susan. "In fact, we have a whole house. Would have even more if you two moved out."

"Twat," Daisy muttered, heading back upstairs.

Ian polished off his breakfast with savage enthusiasm, belched loudly enough to set the plates rattling in the cupboard, and wiped his mouth on the back of his hand. "Gotta get shot of this bloody thing," he grumbled to himself, checking his Rolex as he waddled toward the front door.

Tolstoy trotted after him, snuffling affectionately.

"See you tonight my boy," he told the dog as he left for work.

The tedious journey to work on the train was as uneventful as ever.

Ian shuffled into Post Office HQ, scanning the first floor and then the second instinctively. No sign of Alison. Good. He made himself a catastrophic cup of tea – more milk than tea, scalding hot – and sploshed it across his desk. He dabbed it up with a sheet of photocopying paper, which he threw into the recycling bin. The place smelled like it always did: burnt toner, despair, and stale biscuits.

He slouched toward the toilets. Once inside the cubical Ian locked the door, perched awkwardly on the closed toilet seat, and pulled out his secure phone. A single message awaited him.

*IS THIS YOUR ALISON?*

He opened the attachment. It hit him like a hammer. A photo: Alison, sitting on the edge of a hospital bed, holding hands with the gelded gym trainer – the one Ian had, creatively speaking, 'discouraged' from dabbling with his wife – smiling tenderly, even lovingly at one another. Ian's stomach twisted.

He texted back with shaking fingers: *Jeez! Yes, that's her. Shocked! How could I be so gullible?*

The reply came within seconds: *She's just good. Like you. Both long-term embeds. She was here to observe and potentially neutralise you.*

Ian leaned back against the cold tiled wall, letting the phone slide into his lap. He felt something like grief, but sharper. Betrayal with a twist of bitterness. He texted again, dry humour a last defence:

*And I really thought she fancied me...*

The screen answered with a single lol emoji.

He flushed the toilet, shoved the phone into his pocket, and marched back to his desk – deflated and depressed.

Eventually Alison arrived, glowing as ever, breezing through the rows of cubicles. "Sorry I am late," she said, plopping down across from him with a smile. "Visiting an old friend of mine with... well...prostate problems." Ian raised an eyebrow. "Oh... sorry to hear that. Hope he's okay? It can be nasty that," Ian concluded – trying to look impassive.

"They had to operate," she said, sipping her tea. "But he'll live."

There was a long pause. Then:

"You don't have a Russian doppelgänger, do you?" Alison asked lightly.

Ian froze for half a second, then forced a chuckle. "Eh?" he grunted, feigning ignorance.

"I saw someone last night. Spitting image of you. Younger. Sharper suit. Dashingly mysterious. Speaking Russian."

Ian laughed, spraying crumbs everywhere. "So, nothing like me at all then."

Alison laughed too, leaning in slightly.

Ian played the idiot perfectly. Then he struck. "Hey," he said casually. "I've got a free night tonight. Fancy a drink or dinner?"

Alison's eyes lit up. "Really? I'd love to!" she said eagerly. "The Banker's Draught Pub, Near Bank Station, 7:30?"

"Perfect," Ian said, flashing his best goofy grin. "See where the evening takes us..." As Alison drifted away quickly toward the toilets, Ian leaned back, arms folded behind his head. "Contacting her handler for advice, I'd bet my fortune on it," Ian muttered He smiled grimly. *Let her come*, he thought.

Ian left work early, so that he could go to his penthouse to prepare.

The lift doors opened directly into the heart of the penthouse, and the hush greeted Ian like an old friend — one who didn't need to speak, didn't need to ask questions, and didn't care that you hadn't shaved or killed someone again.

The air was cool and faintly citrus-scented, the sharp edge of lemon peel riding over a deeper base of cedar and dry tobacco – the room's own cologne, curated and subtle. It clung to the drapes and the floorboards. It had history.

Ian stepped inside and exhaled through his nose. No wife. No dog. No questions. Just stillness and soft lighting and the quiet hum of a place that didn't pretend to be a home. The penthouse wasn't for living in – it was for functioning. For shape shifting. For slipping out of one skin and into another.

He walked through the main living area, ignoring the panoramic view of the London City skyline slowly goldening in the west. The horizon glowed like theatre lights behind smoked glass, but Ian barely glanced at it. He was already loosening his tie with one hand and stepping out of his shoes with the other, leaving a faint trail of crumpled, lived-in banality across the sleek polished parquet flooring.

His work clothes hit the floor in a soft, defeated pile – synthetic trousers, a shirt with curry stains, and socks that should have been put out of their misery years ago.

He stood in his pants for a moment and scratched absently at his belly, staring at the wardrobe. Then, slowly and with the care of a craftsman returning to his bench, Ian began to arm himself. The first layer was a soft, charcoal-grey undershirt – breathable, form-fitting. Over it, he pulled on a bullet and stab-resistant vest, the fabric thick but flexible, tailored to disappear beneath looser layers. It moulded against him like old muscle memory.

From a hidden drawer behind a false panel, he selected his weapons with the reverence some men reserve for vinyl records or handmade razors: two spring-loaded daggers, identical, their blades blackened and folded into wrist straps. He slid them onto his wrists beneath the cuffs of his shirt. Twin pistols, compact and matte black, suppressors already screwed on. They were lightweight but serious – the kind of weapons that didn't shout; they whispered. He checked both chambers with a lazy flick of the thumb, holstered them under each armpit, and tugged the shirt down to cover them. A muted grey – casual, untucked, soft enough to drape naturally over steel – but not too smart. He would need to fit some of his normal work clothes over the top – to avoid raising suspicion.

He stared at his reflection in the mirror. Then, without ceremony, he removed the Rolex Daytona from his wrist – still gleaming from the hotel job – and placed it back in its velvet cradle. He reached for his faithful, battered Casio instead: the face scratched, the plastic strap held together with a paperclip. He clipped it to his wrist like a lucky charm and rolled his sleeves up slightly, enough to look relaxed. Not far enough to show the razor-sharp steel lurking beneath them.

He moved to the bar cart and poured a small measure of a very special 50-year-old Glenfarclas into a cut-glass tumbler, letting the deep amber liquid coat the inside his mouth like varnish. He sipped once, no more. Just enough to settle the nerves that wouldn't come anyway.

It was difficult knowing he was going to have to kill Alison. He had really liked her...a lot! But the stark realisation had come home to roost – she was simply the same as him, a conniving, ruthless killer.

He stood in the middle of the room, dressed like an off-duty geography teacher with two silent pistols and the ability to kill a man – or woman – with a choice of two spring-loaded razor-sharp daggers.

He felt both sad and angry about Alison and what he now knew he had to do. It was almost funny. Almost.

Ian checked his phone (the encrypted one). Time to go. He turned off the lights. The penthouse now dark behind him – holding its breath – waiting for his safe return later, once the job was done.

He felt a tinge of apprehension as he walked out onto the dark street. It was raining. Threadneedle Street at night had a strange, hollow calm – the city's financial heart exhaling after a day of tension, transaction, and silent contempt. The suits were gone now, dispersed to taxis, trains, private clubs, or anonymous flats stacked like filing cabinets above the Northern line. The buildings loomed overhead in sober stone and polished glass, as if even the architecture were auditing you.

The streetlamps glowed orange against the drizzle. Traffic hissed. A few pedestrians shuffled past, shoulders hunched, collars up, lost in their phones or the weight of their overdrafts. There were CCTV domes overhead, a scattering of cleaners in high-vis vests, and that particular quiet you only get in financial districts after working hours — sterile, expensive, and just a little bit ghostly.

Ian paused at the corner, eyes sweeping the junction. He didn't look like he was watching – but he was. Doorways. Reflections. Angles. Blind spots.

No shadows moved where they shouldn't. No footsteps stuck to his rhythm. No watchers. No tails. Excellent.

He adjusted his jacket, shifted the weight of the pistols beneath each arm, and stepped off the kerb.

The Bankers Draught pub squatted halfway down the block like an old, resentful drunk. It looked like it had been built before decimalisation and hadn't had a proper clean since. The black-painted fascia bore the name in tired gold lettering, slightly peeling, with a faint halo of pigeon shit giving the 'R' a jaunty little hat. Its windows were fogged up with condensation, streaked with fingerprints and the shadows of people hunched over drinks. You couldn't see in from the street, which was half the point. The signage in the window promised a 'Generous Happy Hour' and 'Famous Steak Pie' in fading white marker pen. Someone had drawn a crude Union Jack below it with the confidence of someone who'd failed art GCSE twice. The front door was sticky to the touch and heavier than it looked. Ian stepped inside.

The smell hit him first – warm beer, stale carpet, old leather, and whatever they used to mop the floors that somehow made them dirtier. It was the kind of pub that lived in the Venn diagram between authentic charm and a food hygiene warning. At lunchtime a bustling ale house for City traders and insurance brokers, in the evening mostly deserted apart from drunken young brokers who had made an afternoon of it.

It was slightly dark inside. Not atmospheric-dark – just badly lit. The overhead fixtures buzzed with ageing bulbs, casting a jaundiced glow on the worn carpet, which was patterned in maroon swirls and grey stains that might have once been a design.

The bar ran around in an oval, heavy oak worn smooth by generations of elbows, with dozens of hand pumps and a cracked mirror behind the bar either side. It made everyone look ten years older and ten pints deeper. A chalkboard listed guest ales in illegible scrawl. Glasses hung from an overhead rack, mostly clean. Someone had once told Ian that it had originally been an actual bank branch – but Ian didn't know if this was true.

Behind the bar, the landlord – a bearded man with the shoulders of an ex-rugby player and the attitude of someone who'd had enough of your nonsense before you'd even opened your mouth – nodded at Ian with the glazed warmth of familiarity or boredom. Probably a bit of both, to be honest.

The remaining patrons were what you'd expect at this hour and postcode: a few solitary pint-sippers reading their newspapers; a cluster of off-duty traders and brokers in rolled-up shirts and loosened ties, red-faced and swearing too loudly; and a lone woman near the back working her way through a large rosé and a bag of porkscratchings like she had nothing left to lose.

The music was a faint hum from a Bluetooth speaker behind the bar. Ian recognised it was a Bored Vikings track that he liked – 'Music that stabs and wounds'. *Very appropriate,* he thought to himself, considering what was about to happen.

Ian moved to a booth near the back, beneath a wall-mounted flatscreen, showing Sky News on mute. The subtitles were three seconds behind the presenter's mouth, and no one was watching. He sat with his back to the wall, line of sight on both doors and the bar. One hand casually near his lap, close to the knife tucked under his shirt. Just in case.

A waitress in a stretched polo shirt came over.

"Drink?"

"Pint of Guinness," Ian said. "And a packet of peanuts. Salted."

She nodded and vanished without expression.

He exhaled slowly and took in the room again.

Low threat. No signals. He checked his watch – the battered Casio ticking steadily, comfortably, on his wrist. Now all he had to do...was wait.

Alison arrived right on time, smiling, radiant. "Hi Ian!" she said brightly. "You look...very you. Very nice."

"You must be mad," Ian said, standing to pull out her chair.

"But I'm happy to humour you."

They drank. Laughed. And ate – home-made pies and double cooked chips. If Ian didn't know better, he would have thought they were having a great time.

Ian spilled gravy down his shirt. Picked his nose discreetly. Scratched in places polite men don't generally scratch in mixed company.

Alison remained perfect as always – patient, amused, flirtatious. If she noticed Ian's act, she gave no sign.

Later, Alison leaned in.

"A friend of mine is away," she said coyly. "I've got the keys to her flat. If you fancy a late-night coffee there?"

Ian smiled, sheepish. "I won't say no to a snifter. But I'd prefer somewhere more neutral," he said. "Safer for both of us."

Alison looked surprised – maybe genuinely – but nodded. "Sure. That makes sense," she said.

Ian told Alison about a budget hotel he knew nearby and suggested they tried there.

When they arrived, Ian realised it was a bit less salubrious than he had remembered. Well, he hadn't been there for years.

The hotel had once had aspirations. Probably in the mid-'70s, when brown tiles and artex ceilings were still allowed. Now it just smelled. The faint tang of disinfectant failing to cover the scent of overuse and things best left unspoken. The carpet in the lobby was threadbare and mottled with what looked like decades of boot polish, spilled coffee, and human shame. A dusty artificial plant slouched in the corner beside a vending machine that hummed ominously, stocked with lukewarm Fanta and a lone, dented can of Lilt that had probably seen a Labour government come and go.

Ian and Alison stood at the check-in desk, saying nothing. They weren't holding hands. They weren't laughing. They weren't the kind of couple that hotel staff remembered – and that was entirely the point.

Ian handed over the ID and the cash with casual efficiency. Alison signed the register with a flick of her wrist. The receptionist – a pale man with a wispy goatee and the aura of someone who had given up asking questions of mismatched couples back in 2006 – didn't even look up. Just slid across a keycard and pointed at a laminated sign about breakfast hours and smoking fines. "Room 104," he muttered, voice cracked from too many nights spent swallowing other people's noise.

"Cheers," Ian replied, pocketing the brass key.

They turned without another word. The lift was broken – of course – so they climbed the narrow staircase, their footsteps muffled by the spongy, wine-coloured carpet that gave slightly underfoot, like stepping on forgotten sponge cake. The banister wobbled when Ian touched it.

Alison was silent, her expression unreadable. Not tense. Not relaxed. Somewhere in between. Coiled.

Ian matched her pace, one hand casually resting at his side, fingers brushing the hem of his untucked shirt close to where a pistol nestled cold against his ribs.

The corridor on the first floor was a long, dim passage lit by tired sconces that cast amber blotches on the floral wallpaper. The pattern had once been cheerful – tiny yellow flowers and blue vines but time, smoke, and careless elbows had turned it into something more abstract. Water stains bloomed across the ceiling in Rorschach shapes that no one wanted to interpret. A low electrical buzz filled the air – the sound of a cheap transformer somewhere in the building struggling to stay alive. Every now and then, a door creaked in the distance, or a muffled laugh echoed from behind thin walls. Somewhere, far off, a plumbing pipe let out a slow, metallic groan like a dying walrus. There was also – unmistakably – the faint, rhythmic thud of a headboard meeting plasterboard, accompanied by occasional moaning. Not particularly enthusiastic. More contractual. Everyone was at it Ian thought!

Alison glanced sideways but said nothing.

Ian smirked.

"Nice place," he muttered. "Romantic. Real murder-suicide vibes."

Alison allowed herself a faint smile, but her eyes stayed razor sharp.

They reached Room 104, halfway down the corridor. The door was chipped around the handle and had been painted over so many times it looked embalmed. The number was slightly crooked.

Ian slid in the key and unlocked the door slowly. He pushed the door open. "After you," he said.

She stepped inside first. He followed – and let the door swing behind them.

The hallway buzzed with the faint hum of bad wiring and the occasional coital moan from somewhere deep within the building.

The moment her heels clicked on the cheap laminate floor, he followed, pulling the door closed behind them with a muted thud. The latch slid into place, followed by the soft metallic clatter of the safety chain being drawn tight. Ian turned the key in the lock too – just to make sure there could be no interruptions.

For a moment there was silence. A flickering halogen bulb overhead cast shadows on the threadbare carpet. The room smelled of old fabric, cheaper soap, and a faint trace of mildew rising from the bathroom tiles. Alison turned to him and smiled. Not a warm smile. Not a flirty one. The smile of a woman who'd just remembered her orders.

And then – smooth as glass – she reached into her coat and drew a semi-automatic pistol. Small. Compact. Snub nosed. Suppressor already fitted ready to dish out death.

She raised it without hesitation.

Ian moved on reflex.

His arm snapped up and batted her wrist sideways with a sickening crack of bone-on-bone. The gun skittered across the floor, bouncing once before vanishing under the sagging sofa in the room.

She didn't flinch. Instead, she pivoted on her heel and brought her foot crashing into Ian's side – a roundhouse kick of some sort that hammered into his ribs like a sledgehammer wrapped in leather. A shock of pain bloomed across his chest, white-hot and electric. He staggered but stayed upright.

"Bloody hell," he grunted, winded. "That's a solid six out of ten."

Alison's follow-through was already in motion. She raised her leg again – but Ian, breath hissing between his teeth, grabbed her ankle mid-swing.

"Gotcha," he rasped.

He yanked, attempting to crack her like a whip. She twisted mid-air, somehow rolling with the fall – her spine thudding hard against the thin carpet – but she tucked, turned, and rolled smoothly into a crouch. One hand shot under the sofa. Fingers closed around the gun. She came up quick – too quick – barrel aimed centre-mass.

Oh! She was good!

Ian closed the gap in half a heartbeat. He slammed his hand down on her wrist again, forcing the muzzle up just as it barked once – a muffled "phfft" that popped the lightbulb above and showered the room in darkness, glass and sparks.

Then the fight went feral.

Ian pinned her arm and drove her backwards into the wall. The plaster gave with a wet crack, a fist-sized crater left behind where her shoulder hit. Alison snarled, baring her teeth like a wolf. Barked. Howled. And yelped!

"Now," Ian said, panting, their faces inches apart. "That's the foreplay over with."

She drove her knee into his thigh – hard, right above the knee joint. His leg buckled. He hissed in pain and staggered sideways, catching himself on a rickety desk – 1930's mock Tudor. A lamp crashed to the floor and shattered.

She surged forward again. This time with her bare hands. She launched into a spinning elbow aimed at his temple. Ian ducked, barely, the strike grazing the top of his head. He retaliated with a headbutt of his own – short, brutal – his forehead cracking against the bridge of her nose. Blood spurted.

She stumbled back, blinking, swiping it away with the back of her sleeve.

Then she came again. They collided like rugby forwards in a pub car park. She clawed for his holsters – found one – tried to draw. Ian caught her wrist and twisted it hard. She let out a low growl, brought her forehead down. in a headbutt of her own – stars burst behind Ian's eyes.

They crashed into the bathroom door. It burst open. The towel rail snapped off the wall as they tumbled inside.

They slipped on the wet tiles. She went down first. He landed on top of her. She headbutted him again. Harder. He reeled. She kneed him in the crotch – enough to hurt, not enough to stop him.

Alison moved like a viper: low, fast, and surgical. No wasted motion. No rage. Just a frightening, practised economy of violence honed over the years. Her hands were fists, but her whole body was a weapon – knees, elbows, head, shoulder. Everything designed to break, disable, or kill.

Ian countered the only way he knew how: not with grace, but with brute experience. The kind of muscle memory that comes from shisha bars in Fallujah, alleyways in Bratislava, stairwells in Aleppo. His style was ugly – all elbows, headbutts, and sheer bloody persistence – but it had kept him alive for three decades, and he wasn't about to start losing to someone who still moisturised.

"Let's go for a walk," he growled, and drove her backward into the bathroom wall with a force that would have knocked the sense out of a lesser human. The wall buckled and part gave way. They crashed through in a spray of plasterboard and perished paint, the frame behind snapping under their combined weight. They tumbled back onto the tiled floor in a tangle of limbs and rage. The sink caught Alison across the back. With a brittle crack, the ceramic pedestal snapped clean in half. Porcelain fragments rained down like confetti. Water gushed from an exposed pipe, spraying water across the floor like arterial blood. It hit the far wall, pooling fast. The air filled with the sharp tang of cold metal and old grout. Ian reached for one of his spring-loaded wrist blades, thumbed the trigger.

Nothing. Jammed. Damn!

She grabbed the edge of the shattered mirror on the wall and slashed at him with a shard the size of a kitchen knife. It missed his throat by inches and catching his jacket lapel. He grabbed her by the neck – not to choke, but to hold her still – and slammed her head against the edge of the bath. Once. Twice.

Her grip faltered. The glass shard in her hand dropped.

Ian hauled himself up, panting like a steam engine, blood dripping from his eyebrow, shirt torn open. Moving towards the bedroom.

She was still moving. Of course she was. She drove her elbow straight between his shoulder blades, sending him sprawling face-first into the cheap MDF chest of drawers beside the bed. It exploded into fragments – a Gideon's Bible and a TV remote control went flying in all directions.

Ian coughed hard. Something cracked in his ribs. Definitely not for the first time.

She was already on him again. Three punches – one to the throat, one to the kidney, one aimed high at his temple. He ducked the last, barely, but the others hit home. Pain flared behind his eyes. His vision went white for a split second.

He caught her elbow mid-swing on the return – sheer instinct – and pivoted hard, using her own momentum against her. Both rolled.

Ian landed on top of Alison on the bed, barely conscious. The crook of her forearm dug under his chin, clamping down on his windpipe with surgical precision. Her bicep pressing the arteries either side of his neck. A proper blood choke. A sleeper hold done right. Professional. Intimate. Final.

Ian thrashed, boots kicking uselessly against the wet carpet. His fingers clawed at her wrist, at her elbow – anywhere he could get leverage.

The edges of his vision began to pulse. Black spots gathered like shadows under a door. His limbs were growing heavier by the second. His lungs screamed. Every nerve shouted for oxygen.

Then – close to his ear – Alison whispered, soft and almost affectionate: "You should've stayed a slob, Ian."

Sensing that this moment was his last chance to survive, Ian's hand found the other wrist trigger. This one worked.

Click. Snap.

The blade shot out from his right wrist – a silent, surgical whisper – and buried itself deep into the side of Alison's skull.

Her body tensed. Then shuddered.

Her eyes went wide. Lips parted. Then slackened. Then stilled.

She blinked once. Her lips parted like she might say something. Then her eyes glazed, the colour draining like someone pulling a curtain.

Ian lay there for a moment, chest heaving, ribs screaming.

Through the paper-thin wall, a couple mid-coitus in the next room had heard the frantic and very noisy activity of Ian and Alison – imagining it was a full-on sex session between a very passionate couple with a tiger in their tank.

"Christ," the man whispered. "That sounds intense."

"I wish we sounded like that," the woman muttered back.

Ian let his head drop back onto the torn mattress, blood trickling into his collar. "Bloody hell," he croaked. He exhaled. And just stared at the ceiling.

The couple next door had now stopped their lovemaking entirely.

"...Jesus Christ," the man whispered.

"I told you we should've gone to the Travelodge," the woman hissed at him.

Apart from the distant drip of water, the soft buzz of faulty electrics, and the buzz in his ears there was complete and utter silence.

Ian wiped his mouth on the sleeve of his ruined shirt and lay still, the scent of blood, cheap soap, and cordite thick in the air around him. The room looked like a bomb blast had married a flood and divorced reality. Total devastation.

The mattress was half-off its frame, springs poking out like snapped ribs. One leg of the bed had splintered, making it tilt at an odd, accusatory angle. The chest of drawers was collapsed in a heap of laminate and fake brass handles, its drawers cracked like fallen coffins, leaking folded towels and a laminated emergency fire plan. Water gushed from the shattered bathroom pipe, still spitting rhythmically into the widening pool that had spread across the floorboards and into the bedroom. The entire carpet squelched with each breath the room seemed to take. The flickering wall sconce sparked occasionally, throwing shadows across cracked plaster and blood-smeared tiles. The sink lay in two jagged halves against the tub. The bathtub itself – tilted, holding several inches of water, blood, and silence.

Ian stood at the far end of the room, leaning heavily on what remained of the wardrobe door. His shirt hung open, soaked and torn; one sleeve ripped off at the elbow. The blood from a cut above his eyebrow had slowed but not stopped. Dried blood had formed a crust along the side of his nose.

He moved stiffly, like someone who had just escaped a car crash. Ribs burning. Leg bruised. Hands still shaking slightly.

And then, with all the urgency of a bored civil servant filing paperwork, Ian reached into the inner pocket of his ruined shirt and pulled out his secure phone – the black, unmarked one. The screen lit up. He thumbed out a message.

*ROOM 104. Big clean-up required. Job done.*

He stared at the screen for a second, blood still dripping from his hand onto the touchscreen. Then hit send.

He waited.

The reply came back almost instantly.

*Understood. Cleaners will deal with it. Lock the door and leave. Jim has dealt with the gelding.*

Ian let out a weak, gravelled chuckle. It caught in his throat and turned into a cough that bent him double. He spat something red into the corner of the carpet and wiped his mouth on the back of his sleeve.

"Good lad," he croaked, looking around at the wreckage.

There was no glory in it. No victory.

Time to go home...via the Penthouse. To get straighten up a bit.

The street outside the hotel was quiet now – that particular hush that only comes late at night, when the taxis grow sparse and even the night buses sound half-asleep. Ian walked with the slow, deliberate pace of a man held together more by stubbornness than anatomy. His shirt was buttoned wrong. His ribs ached with every breath. His left knee clicked. He didn't limp – not exactly. But the rhythm of his steps had shifted. A half-beat slower. Just enough to suggest something beneath the surface had come loose.

He flagged down a black cab, gave an address near to his penthouse that didn't have CCTV, in a voice like broken gravel, and let his head rest briefly against the cool glass as the city passed by in flickering yellow stripes.

The penthouse lift doors sighed open. Inside, the silence felt clinical. Artificial. Too perfect. No dog. No wife. No dead girl from work bleeding into the floorboards. Just dim lighting, climate control, and the soft hum of money well spent.

Ian stripped out of his ruined clothes with the grace of a medieval soldier peeling away armour. The shirt came off in wet slaps. The trousers sagged with water and plaster dust. His socks had turned pink from someone else's blood, or maybe it was his. Each item he folded once – roughly – and stuffed into a plastic bag labelled in sharpie: DISPOSE. The pistols went into a drawer, followed by the wrist blades. Including the one he had prised loose from Alison's temple. He cleaned and then placed them with care, as though they were precious. Tools, not trophies.

The secure weapons locker shut with a hiss and two beeps.

He stood in the middle of the room in just his Y-fronts, looking like something dredged from the Thames, and padded barefoot across the polished wood floor to the kitchen. The bottle of the very best Glenfarclas was sitting there waiting. He poured two fingers' worth – no ice – and knocked it back in a single swallow, then poured another, slower. This one he sipped, leaning against the granite worktop. With his other hand, he reached into the cupboard and retrieved a crumpled bag of salt and vinegar crisps. They exploded open with a hiss. He ate them in three savage handfuls – stuffing, not chewing – the vinegar stinging a split lip he hadn't noticed until now. He licked his fingers clean and finished the whisky in another neat mouthful.

For a moment, the only sound in the penthouse was his breathing. Steady. Controlled. Like nothing had happened. Like he was just a man coming home from working late at a very dull job in an office. He checked the time: 12:37 a.m.

"Right," he muttered to no one. "Time to go home."

After showering and dressing in clean clothing, Ian took a Black cab to Kings Cross. He'd managed to dress most of his injuries. Once at the station he descended into the tiled bowels of the Underground with his collar up and his bag slung low.

The late train crowd was thin – a few stragglers in work coats, two teenagers with smudged eyeliner, a sleeping man with a pizza box on his lap. He found a seat and took it slowly.

His battered Casio ticked away. His entire body ached. His stomach grumbled, confused by the combination of murder, whisky, and crisps. The train shuddered into motion. Ian leaned his head against the window and closed his eyes – not asleep, but somewhere near it. Dream-adjacent. His reflection in the dark glass stared back at him – not Ian the post office worker, not Ian the killer. Just a tall, tired, overweight man – with food stains and indigestion. Heading home.

Ian was glad to arrive in one piece. Susan was asleep, face soft, mouth slightly open. Ian slid under the covers beside her, every muscle aching.

Tolstoy shifted in his sleep, emitting a gassy sigh.

Ian smiled into the dark. Still alive. Still dangerous. Still Daddy.

## Chapter Seven
# A Man of Taste

*"Always be polite. Especially when planning something deeply impolite."*
**~ The Gentleman Assassin's Pocket Handbook**

# Chapter 7

# A Man of Taste

Breakfast, Ian decided, was a sacred ritual. It was a ceremony, a declaration of personal independence, and occasionally – if you were lucky – a minor culinary war crime. This morning's offering was no exception.

The kitchen counter bore witness to the carnage: a loaf of squashed white bread, a half-empty jar of salad cream, and two family-sized bags of cheese and onion crisps, their contents crumbled and scattered liberally across every available surface.

Ian whistled cheerfully as he worked, slathering the bread with a thick, almost structural layer of Salad Cream before artfully arranging crushed crisps on top. He mashed the two halves together with a flourish, squeezing until the salad cream oozed out of the sides. Daisy wandered in mid-assembly, took one look, and recoiled.

"Oh my God," she said, appalled. "That's not breakfast. That's a hate crime."

"It's an *artisan sarnie,* hand crafted," Ian said proudly. "Crisps and Salad Cream. Bit of crunch, bit of tang. Perfect start to the day."

Susan appeared in the doorway, arms folded, radiating long-suffering exasperation. "What in the name of sanity are you doing, Daddy?" she asked, eyeing the soggy monstrosity in his hands.

Ian beamed. "Just wondering… can you toast Salad Cream sandwiches? Get a bit of a melt going?"

Susan blinked. "Don't be so daft."

Ian considered her words carefully. He held the sandwich at arm's length, peering at it like a biologist examining a particularly aggressive microbe. "Bit of a shame, really," he said. "Could be revolutionary."

Susan sighed, crossing to the kettle to make tea.

Tolstoy, lurking under the table, gave Ian a hopeful wag. Ian dropped a bit of sandwich to the floor. Tolstoy sniffed it, licked it once, and then backed away suspiciously. Even the dog had standards.

Susan slapped a cup of tea down in front of Ian. "Eat it and be gone before you burn the house down."

Ian, unfazed, bit into the sandwich with a loud crunch and a noise that could only be described as sexual satisfaction.

Susan sat opposite him; arms folded, shaking her head. "You've got bruises all on your face Ian, how on earth did you do that?" she asked.

"Tripped on the stairs on the underground and fell down them," Ian replied.

"For heaven's sake, you are completely hopeless!" she replied. "You are a danger to yourself."

The nagging had had started to creep back. Little things. Why his socks were never paired. Why his shaving foam was in the fridge. Why he insisted on referring to crisps as a legitimate food group. It was oddly comforting. Life settling back into its familiar grooves, like a record with a few deep scratches but still willing to play.

Max wandered in, grabbed a banana, and left again – smirking but without comment. Susan raised an eyebrow. "Your children think you're a freak."

Ian chewed thoughtfully. "It's character-building."

He finished the remainder of his sandwich in three heroic bites, wiped his mouth on the sleeve of his jacket, checked his battered Casio, and hauled himself upright. "Off to serve King and Country," he said grandly, grabbing his battered Post Office satchel.

Susan just rolled her eyes. "It's only the Post Office...Try not to lower the tone too much."

Ian grinned. "No promises."

He gave her a quick, messy kiss on the cheek, smearing her with salad cream, and lumbered out the door. The crisp autumn air slapped him awake as he trudged toward the station. The world smelled of damp leaves, distant car fumes, and fresh bakery bread. A solid, boring workday. He was settling. Life was settling. It was almost disappointing.

The Northern Line rumbled and shuddered, the carriage crammed with commuters pretending they weren't packed into a metal sausage casing of despair.

Ian swayed with the motion; one hand braced on a grubby steel pole. Somewhere in the tangle of bodies, a phone pinged. It wasn't his public phone. It was the other one. The real one. He fished it from his inner pocket, shielding the screen with his body.

A new message: *ASSET TWO-NINE: Continue monitoring Malcolm Duffy. Possible deep embed. Proceed with extreme caution.*

Ian sighed. He tucked the phone away.

Of course, life couldn't stay normal. Not for him. What was he thinking?

Ian exited the station into a wall of city noise: the endless shriek of buses, the low thrum of taxis, the cackle of pigeons bullying tourists. He walked fast; shoulders hunched against the chill. For the first time in a while, he felt heavy.

No more Alison. He couldn't shake her from his mind. Her laugh. The way she leaned in when she spoke. The sharp glint behind her smile. He had genuinely liked her, in his own battered, hopeless way. And now she was dead. Killed by him. He told himself it was part of the job. Collateral damage. It was either her or him. But part of him still grieved slightly. Even if he couldn't show it.

Ruth, his boss, intercepted him before he even made it to his desk. She was vibrating with nerves, hair frazzled, lipstick slightly smeared. "Ian," she said, grabbing his arm. "My office. Now."

He let himself be steered into the large office, more curious than worried. Ruth closed the door carefully. "I'm not great at... well... this sort of thing," she said, wringing her hands. "But I thought you should hear it from me."

Ian's stomach dropped. He schooled his face into polite concern.

"It's Alison," Ruth said, voice cracking slightly. "There was a car accident late last night. She's... she didn't make it." She looked at him, wide-eyed, expecting a reaction.

Ian tried. He really did. He screwed up his face, focused hard on squeezing out a single, dignified tear. Nothing. Just a faint twitch, like he was suppressing a sneeze.

Ruth gave him an awkward pat on the shoulder. "I know you had a... well kind of a... fondness for her," she said gently. "So if you need a few days off... compassionate leave, totally fine. In fact, take a week if you... erm... need to."

Ian nodded gravely. "Thank you," he said, voice just the right amount of hoarse. "I think I will."

Ruth beamed, relieved to have survived the emotional minefield.

Ian shuffled out of the room; head bowed respectfully. He kept it up all the way down the hall. The moment he was out of sight, he grinned broadly. A few days off, maybe a week, legitimately. Maybe he could spin it out to 10 days? Time to deal with Mr. Duffy.

Ian went straight back home. Well, kind of straight back home. He loitered outside his own house for a moment, scanning the street. Malcolm Duffy's house looked utterly unremarkable. Small. Semi-detached. Brown pebble-dash exterior. A neat row of chrysanthemums in the garden. No suspicious blacked-out windows. No strange satellite dishes. Just...well normal. Which made it even more suspicious.

Ian smoothed down his jacket, pasted on a friendly smile, and marched across to Duffy's front door. He rang the bell. Then the door creaked open. And there he was. Malcolm Duffy. Mid-fifties. Narrow-shouldered. Thinning hair parted with obsessive precision. A cream-coloured sweater vest stretched over a shirt that was buttoned all the way to the top but clearly hadn't seen daylight in a while. He wore spectacles that magnified his watery grey eyes until they looked like dinner plates – complete with trembling reflections. A man who looked like he'd once tried to make conversation at a model train exhibition and been politely ignored.

Ian smiled – wide, toothy, and just the wrong side of charming.

The house was almost aggressively neat. White uPVC windows, scrubbed to hospital brightness. Hanging baskets with suspiciously symmetrical petunias. A laminated "NO COLD CALLERS" sign taped to the letterbox, and a brass door knocker shaped like a flying duck polished within an inch of its life. Even the welcome mat looked new – or at least recently hoovered and cleaned.

Ian stood on the step in his creased clothing, holding a packet of shop-bought shortbread that had expired last March. The 'neighbourly' gift was mostly a prop – an excuse to loiter long enough for a proper look.

"Hello there! Ian, from up the road," he said, pointing vaguely over his shoulder. "Thought it was about time we met properly. Figured I'd bring over something for you as a gift – gesturing towards the shortbread. Always nice to know who's keeping an eye on your bins."

Malcolm blinked slowly. His lips parted as if he was waiting for a prompt. "Oh," he said at last, voice thin and reedy, like it came from a throat that didn't often volunteer sound. "Right. Hello." He glanced down at the shortbread, then back up at Ian as if trying to work out if this was some kind of elaborate ruse.

Ian extended a hand.

Malcolm looked at it like it might explode. Then, with visible reluctance, he reached out and gave it a single limp shake – the handshake equivalent of a wet paper towel.

"Come in, if you like," Malcolm murmured. "I've just boiled the kettle." He stepped back into the hallway, and Ian followed him in. And stopped dead.

The smell hit Ian first – lavender polish and something fainter underneath: dust, starch, the precise aroma of a life that probably hadn't deviated from schedule in twenty years. The front room opened up like a pensioner's dollhouse – low-ceilinged, over-warm, and aggressively beige. A gas fire hummed in the hearth even though it was pushing twenty-one degrees outside. Net curtains filtered the daylight into a kind of bureaucratic haze. And everywhere – on every single surface – sat dogs. Rows of them. Not real ones. Staffordshire ceramic dogs. Dozens of them. Possibly even hundreds. They stared out from shelves, mantels, glass-fronted cabinets, and wall-mounted ledges. Some stood proud on lace doilies. Others lurked beneath potted ferns or peeked around framed photos that had faded into pink-tinged oblivion. Big dogs. Medium sized dogs. Tiny dogs. Glossy white ones with high gloss black muzzles and disturbing human eyes. Spaniels with painted gold chains around their necks. Terriers with blue bows. Whippets, greyhounds, pugs. A few were cracked and carefully glued, repaired with the reverence usually reserved for heirloom china in the great stately homes, or medieval relics in museums. Some sat up straight, their paws neat and symmetrical, expressions fixed in ceramic judgement. Others looked like they'd just heard something deeply alarming.

Ian stood in the doorway, trying to process it all.

Malcolm closed the door behind him and flushed slightly, tugging at the hem of his jumper like a boy caught with a dirty magazine. "I collect them," he said unnecessarily, already moving toward a small side table where a particularly proud looking glazed bulldog stood watch over a stack of Radio Times back issues. I mean who even bothers with the Radio Times these days – the printed edition?

Ian, who had once driven a ballpoint pen through a North Korean agent's neck and used the same pen to sign a hotel check-in slip five minutes later, found himself genuinely – profoundly – at a loss for words.

He cleared his throat. "They're... very lifelike," he offered helpfully. Malcolm's face lit up like a child on Christmas morning. "They are, aren't they? I think so too." he said and crossed to a narrow cabinet with a mirrored back. He opened it reverently, reached in with both hands, and retrieved a porcelain spaniel so delicate it looked like it might sigh if handled too roughly. "This one's Gladys," he said, turning it slowly. "Late Victorian. 1891. See the rose detailing on the collar? That was done with a single brush stroke. Remarkable work. Done by a Staffordshire great! The eyes look so real too."

Ian nodded, mouth twitching into a smile he hoped passed for 'delighted' rather than 'deeply alarmed'.

"Each one tells a story," Malcolm added softly, stroking the spaniel like a real pet. Ian's brain was already cataloguing the layout: no visible cameras, one visible exit, two glasses on the sideboard (one used recently), and a small footstool that could definitely conceal a pressure-trigger bomb or a concealed firearm. Or, of course, even more ceramic dogs.

He made his way toward the sofa – an elderly floral number that looked like it might wheeze if sat on too firmly. He lowered himself between a porcelain golden retriever and a bulldog with a chipped ear. Both stared at him with mute disapproval.

He placed the shortbread on the coffee table, which groaned faintly under its current ceramic population.

"So, Malcolm," Ian said, fishing with the gentle rhythm of a man unspooling bait into still water, "what do you do for work?"

Malcolm smiled, the kind of smile that deflated rather than expanded. "Accountant," he said. "Though I'm retired now. Gave it up a few years ago. Too many spreadsheets. I like things... simple, ordered."

"Simple's underrated," Ian said, still scanning the room without moving his head. There was a clock ticking somewhere. Not a digital one. A proper tick. He wondered if it was counting down to something.

Malcolm sat across from him, clutching Gladys on his lap, stroking her, legs crossed neatly like a man being interviewed for a local paper. "Do you have a hobby, Ian?" he asked.

Ian smiled. "I work in marketing," he said. "So almost anything without buzzwords is a hobby to me these days."

Malcolm nodded sagely, as if this made sense. He reached for a coaster, placed it in front of Ian with ceremonial care. He fetched the tea some moments later – lukewarm, over brewed, and poured into an old Queen's Jubilee mug with too much milk. Simple. Except none of this felt simple.

Ian sipped, eyes never quite leaving Malcolm. Somewhere in the quiet hum of lavender, ticking clocks and staring ceramic spaniels, something didn't add up. And Ian Taylor – freelance assassin, tea-drinker, shortbread biscuit-bringer – intended to find out exactly what.

Ian drank the weak, lukewarm tea Malcolm had pressed into his hand and surveyed the sea of ceramic dogs with growing despair. Polite interest had carried him through the first two minutes. Now he was running on fumes.

"So many... breeds," Ian said lacking the will to continue for much longer, gesturing vaguely at a shelf stacked with tiny, glowering terriers and spaniels.

Malcolm beamed. "Each one unique," he said proudly. "I've catalogued them all. Alphabetical order. Cross-referenced by kennel club standards. All on a series of spreadsheets, with pivots – so I can analyse who painted them and which pottery made them."

Ian nodded as if this was a reasonable use of anyone's finite existence.

"And you've got a lovely garden," Ian offered, fishing for a polite exit from the dog collection.

Malcolm's face lit up like a Christmas tree. "Would you like to see it?"

Ian opened his mouth to decline – but Malcolm was already bustling toward the back door, his excitement dragging Ian along like a fast river current. Malcolm led the way through the narrow side passage with the primness of a diplomat escorting royalty through Versailles. The back door squeaked once on its hinges, then clicked shut behind them. And there it was, in all its parochial, perfect glory. The garden.

If the front of the house was suburban restraint, the rear was full-blown horticultural monomania. Ian stepped into a space that looked less like a garden and more like the back cover of a National Trust brochure, or possibly a set for a period drama where someone was about to die tragically among the delphiniums. It was immaculate. Lawn cut into perfect military stripes. Borders weeded to perfection. A rockery in one corner that had been arranged with near-religious precision — every stone placed like a chess piece; every alpine flower labelled with a tiny, engraved tag. The hedges had been sculpted into precise, formal shapes – cubes, spheres, a few low pyramids that looked suspiciously like miniature missile silos. Not a single leaf out of place. No overhang. No moss. The rose bushes were arranged by bloom colour and date of first flowering. Tiny blackboards stuck into the soil carried hand-written notes like: Climbing Iceberg — deadheaded 11/3. Ian noticed one with a laminated sign reading: DO NOT TOUCH. SENSITIVE ROOT MEMORY.

There was a pergola wrapped in honeysuckle, its scent sweet and vaguely oppressive in the warm air. Beneath it, a cast-iron bench and a small side table, positioned like a viewing platform for a private performance of Gardeners' World: The Operatic Cut.

Malcolm took a deep breath, clearly inhaling the scent of pride and bone meal. "I find the back garden is where one's soul settles," he said.

Ian looked around and privately disagreed – if anything, it felt more like where one's body might be discreetly buried. The shrubs were another matter entirely. So many shrubs. A borderline militarised presence of shrubs. Some tall and stately like guards at Buckingham Palace. Others low, dense and humming with bees. Variegated leaves. Japanese hollies. Ornamental maples. Ian wasn't sure if he was in a back garden or a very polite botanical ambush.

Malcolm gestured grandly to one cluster. "That's my Fothergilla major," he said with the authority of a man unveiling a masterpiece. "American witch alder. The autumn colour? Spectacular. Crisp golds. Warm orange. Hints of rust. Smells faintly of honey, if you get close enough."

Ian, who had once dismantled a sniper rifle with wild honey on his fingers and up his arms, nodded appreciatively.

"Beautiful," he lied.

"And over here," Malcolm continued, marching towards a blood-red tangle of stems, "my prized Euonymus alatus. 'Burning bush,' they call it. Turns a proper inferno red come October. Needs acidic soil, mind you. I adjust the PH with crushed eggshells and sulphur powder." He said it like a man confessing to liking jazz.

Ian followed, stepping carefully around a barrow filled with what looked like precision-sifted mulch. He nodded again, suppressing a massive yawn that nearly unhooked his jaw. He would rather:

Wrestle Tolstoy after feeding him an entire ox liver.

Give a TED Talk on mailshot segmentation.

Be tasered in the testicles by a blindfolded intern.

"And here," Malcolm said, pointing to another glossy-leafed monster, "is my Mahonia japonica. Don't be fooled – she looks friendly but will shred your forearms if you prune her out of season."

"I know the type," Ian muttered, thinking not of the plant but Alison.

It went on.

Latin names. Sunlight ratios. Nitrogen cycles. Soil aeration. Malcolm jabbered with the enthusiasm of a man who hadn't had company since decimalisation. He spoke like a botanical encyclopaedia that had been fed pure espresso and left on autoplay.

Ian checked his Casio discreetly. Four minutes. He could've sworn it had been at least forty. At one point, Malcolm vanished into the greenhouse and returned with a cut stem of something mauve and vaguely medicinal. "Smell this," he said, holding it under Ian's nose. Ian obeyed. It smelled like linseed oil, turps, and whatever it was his mother used to keep under the sink in a tin marked Do Not Touch (1977).

"Lovely," Ian choked out.

Finally – finally – Malcolm slowed. Ran out of Latin names and plant geneses. His shoulders lowered a fraction, like a balloon gently deflating. He turned to Ian, beaming. "You must come again," he said brightly.

"I'd be honoured," Ian replied, with a warmth that should've earned him an Oscar. They shook hands again. Still clammy. Still limp. Still vaguely like touching a half-set jelly. And then Ian fled – through the side gate, across the front path, back toward the beautiful, ordinary, 'normal' mess of his own existence.

As he stepped onto his drive, he muttered to himself: "Either that man's a criminal mastermind..." He paused. Adjusting his frayed shirt cuffs." ...or he's exactly who he says he is, which might be even worse."

Back in the safe embrace of home, Ian leaned against the door for a moment, inhaling the warm, familiar smell of Susan's cooking and Tolstoy's faintly damp fur. He was still smiling when Susan poked her head around the corner.

He told her that he'd just dropped in to visit their neighbour on the way home, to ask him how he kept his roses looking so good.

"And how was it?" she asked dryly.

"Gripping," Ian said. "Roses. Ceramic dogs. Possibly an underground lair filled with death lasers. The normal sort thing with a local criminal mastermind," he answered.

Susan laughed, wiping her hands on a tea towel, dismissing his ridiculous ramblings.

Ian hesitated. "Got some news, Mummy. Some sad news, actually."

She turned, frowning.

"About Alison, at work."

Susan's face shifted – curiosity sharpening into concern.

"She died," Ian said simply. "Car accident."

Susan's hand flew to her mouth in shock.

"Oh, Daddy. I'm so sorry."

Ian shrugged. "Life. One minute you're making plans. The next, you're garden mulch."

Susan crossed the room and hugged him tightly.

He stiffened for a second – then relaxed into it. "Ruth has given me a week off," he added.

That evening, Ian sprawled on the sofa in his pyjamas, a steaming mug of tea balanced precariously on his stomach. The TV burbled in the background: a panel of over-caffeinated presenters arguing about minor celebrities and property prices.

Susan pottered in the kitchen, humming.

Ian, alone for a moment, glanced around guiltily holding a freshly made mug of tea. Then he reached down beside the sofa and unscrewed the flask hidden beneath a cushion. A generous glug of scotch disappeared into the mug. He stirred it with his finger, slurped contentedly, and leaned back.

From the kitchen came Susan's voice: "Daddy, I can *hear* you pouring whisky into your tea!"

Ian took another brazen gulp.

"What are you," he called back, "a cop or something?"

Susan snorted and went back to banging pans.

Ian sank deeper into the sofa, watching a segment about renovating sheds in Suffolk.

He sipped. Sipped again. Warmth spread through his limbs. His eyelids drooped. Ten minutes later, he was fast asleep. Mouth open. Mug still balanced precariously. Until – inevitably – gravity won. Tea and whisky sloshed down his chest, soaking his clothes and leaving a dark, damp stain that slowly expanded like an oil spill. Tolstoy, curled at his feet, didn't even twitch. Domestic bliss. In all its messy, tragic, wonderful glory.

## Chapter Eight
# A Broken Spaniel

*"A good operative keeps two lives. A great one
never lets them meet."*
**~ MI5 Fieldcraft, Volume II**

# Chapter 8

# A Broken Spaniel

If anyone had told Ian Taylor he'd spend the best part of his compassionate leave – well the evenings anyway – hiding in a filthy dirty conifer hedge, with night vision binoculars on, he would have said: "Sounds about right."

It was night four of 'Operation Spaniel'. Ian was crouched in the undergrowth at the edge of his own garden, peering through the murky green glow of his night vision optics. He had told his wife that he was bat watching – after spotting several rare greater mouse-eared bats flying above the garden. She wasn't quite sure what to make of this new interest but decided it was perhaps Ian's way to grieve the loss of Alison – so she just let him get on with it.

Malcolm Duffy's house sat quietly, its curtains drawn, a faint glimmer of light leaking around the edges. At first, Ian had told himself it was just observation. Low-key. Casual. Keep an eye on him, nothing fancy. That lasted about an hour. By the second night, he'd fashioned a camouflage net out of old gardening sheeting and half a dozen plastic pegs.

By the third, he'd started keeping a field notebook, complete with badly drawn diagrams and timings of Malcolm's tea breaks. Now, on the fourth night, he was eating cold pasties out of a rucksack and considering setting up a rota system with Tolstoy.

The houses stood shoulder-to-shoulder like sleepy sentinels, their pebble-dashed facades catching the soft orange spill of the last working streetlamp. Net curtains hung motionless. Garden gnomes grinned stupidly in the dark. A single wind chime tinkled somewhere faintly, out of rhythm with the soft wind driving it.

Cars lined both sides of the road – mostly hatchbacks and sensible estates. A few were draped in half-hearted covers, others glinted faintly under the lamplight: a dusty Volvo, a dented Fiesta with a novelty parking permit, and further down, a high-spec BMW that hadn't moved in three days and probably wasn't taxed – possibly even stolen and neatly abandoned.

Ian crouched low behind a privet hedge, wrapped in a crumpled anorak that smelt faintly of chicken crisps and WD-40. His knees had started to ache forty minutes ago, and the tips of his fingers were beginning to go numb. Tolstoy lay beside him, flat against the cold soil, tail still, ears high. A true professional.

Through the soft fog of his own breath, Ian adjusted his night-vision binoculars, the lenses casting the world in a sickly digital green. His notebook sat open on one knee, biro cap between his teeth. And then – finally – movement.

From the far end of the street, something rolled into view. A dark van. Unmarked. Low-slung. Matte black. Silent as a church mouse.

Its headlights were already off before it drew to a halt, windows tinted to the point of illegality. The engine gave off a faint hum, barely audible – more suggestion than sound – and the tyres moved slow and deliberate, avoiding every pothole, drain and manhole cover like a vehicle and driver that had been trained how not to make any noise when arriving somewhere late at night.

Ian stiffened. Night vision fogged. Heart ticked up.

The van coasted to a stop directly outside Malcolm Duffy's semi-detached fortress of shrubs and Staffordshire porcelain.

The street remained still. No windows twitched. No curtains fluttered. Only Ian and the dog knew something was happening.

Then the driver's door opened with the careful precision of someone who didn't want to be heard.

The man who stepped out was massive. Built like a wardrobe folded into a ski jacket. Six foot five, at least. Shoulders the width of a butcher's counter. A bald head shaved to reflect moonlight and a beard that looked engineered for intimidation. He wore black cargo trousers, heavy boots, and a coat that had far too many pockets for anyone who wasn't either a mercenary or a Lego enthusiast. He moved like a man used to carrying bodies. Or planting them.

In his arms he carried a long, narrow package, wrapped tightly in black canvas and strapped in three places with military tape. It was heavy – Ian could tell by the way the big man had to adjust his grip halfway up the garden path.

A lot of Peonies? A viola? Or a 50-calibre sniper's rifle?

Ian tracked him through the lenses of his night vision binoculars, thumb twitching over his notebook.

The van remained idling – no lights, no driver visible. Probably on a remote kill-switch. Or maybe the kind of van that just disappeared if you blinked at the wrong time.

The bear-man reached the front door and raised one thick, gloved hand.

Knock. Knock.

Two, slow, deliberate knocks that sounded like someone was trying to get Death's attention.

The door opened just wide enough to reveal Malcolm Duffy, dressed in tartan pyjamas and a tartan dressing gown that had seen better centuries. His glasses caught the low light, rendering his eyes into twin moons. He didn't speak. Neither did the bear of a man. No signature. No receipt. No clipboard. Just a single knowing nod. And the parcel was handed over with the care of two people who knew exactly what was inside of it.

Malcolm took it, with a struggle, into the shadows of the hall. The door clicked shut. Lock engaged. Lights stayed off.

The bear-man turned and lumbered back to the van.

He moved with no urgency, no guilt. Just efficiency.

The van eased forward without headlights, turning the corner like a ghost in third gear. Within seconds, it was gone – swallowed into the mist and sodium vapour of suburbia. Ian lowered his binoculars slowly.

Tolstoy gave a soft growl that Ian silenced with a hand on the scruff of his neck. He reached for his pen and scribbled furiously into his notebook:

*01:30 HRS*

*Large male delivery operative – approx. 6'5", bald with Viking-like beard.*

*Eastern European or Scandinavian. Large muscular build*

*Object: long, canvas wrapped. Est. 4.5 feet. Weight approx. 15-20kg*

*No verbal exchange*

*Recipient: Duffy, M. (pyjamas, dressing gown, alert posture)*

*Suspected: deep-cover Soviet logistics OR unnaturally aggressive peony smuggling syndicate*

*Further surveillance required. Possibly with snacks and whisky.*

He underlined the last point twice. Then licked the biro for emphasis and tucked the notebook away.

Tolstoy shifted beside him, tail twitching.

Ian let out a slow breath and whispered, "Let's see what happens next, you porcelain freak." And settled in for the rest of his watch.

This pattern of deliveries became routine.

Almost every night, the bear-man would reappear dropping a mysterious package off.

Sometimes a big parcel, sometimes a small one. Always careful. Always discrete. Always fast.

Malcolm Duffy – supposedly a retired accountant with a ceramic dog fetish – accepted each delivery with the reverence of a priest handling sacred relics.

Ian's instincts buzzed like a broken fire alarm. Something was clearly off. Very off.

The next night, the rain had been falling since just after midnight – the sort of soft, malicious drizzle that didn't so much land on you as absorb into your very soul. The sky hung low, thick with cloud, the moon an afterthought behind shifting veils of grey. The street glistened under the sodium-orange glow of tired streetlamps. Everything looked muted, waterlogged – the kind of evening that even made foxes think twice.

Ian hunkered down deeper into the hedge, the bristling limbs of an overgrown laurel bush pushing damp leaves into his ears and collar. Water trickled down the back of his neck, soaking his second-best parka. His boots were squelching. His notebook was warped. His nose itched. But he was watching intently. Carefully.

His faithful pair of night vision binoculars – high-end, military surplus, probably illegal – were jammed firmly to his face, the world glowing in ghostly green outlines. Duffy's house hovered in the centre of the frame like the subject of a nature documentary: *Here we see the Lesser-Spotted Retired Accountant, rarely observed in the wild, emerging only under cover of fog to fertilise his begonias and possibly orchestrate foreign espionage operations between secret ceramic dog collectors.*

Ian scanned left to right – methodical. Professional. Windows: dark. Front door: closed. Curtains: drawn tight. Rear garden – yikes! His breath caught. There, deep in Duffy's hedgerow, another shape stirred. A hunched figure.

Motionless. Focused. Also holding a pair of night vision binoculars – standard Cold War Russian issue by the looks thought Ian. Ian adjusted his lenses with surgical precision, heart ticking up half a beat. It was Malcolm bloody Duffy!

Crouched among his own shrubs like a sad moss-covered owl, peering directly at Ian through an almost matching pair of night-vision goggles.

Their lenses glowed faintly green in the dark, reflections bouncing off each other like two disco balls locked in a staring contest.

For a moment, neither of them moved. Two middle-aged men. In waterproof coats. Kneeling in separate hedges. Staring at one another through binoculars probably worth more than some people's cars.

Ian felt something deep inside his ribcage shift – a tiny emotional hernia. Not fear. Not even anger. Just a laugh. Pure. Unexpected. Rising like a hiccup in a funeral. He bit it back, hard.

Across the street, Malcolm flinched. Just slightly. Lowered his binoculars a few inches. Rain ran off the peak of his hood. His face was unreadable, but his posture said it all: *Oh God, he's seen me. He's watching me, watching him.*

Initially, Ian didn't so much as blink.

And then – as if choreographed, as if they'd rehearsed it – both men scuttled backwards at the exact same time, retreating into their respective gardens with the graceless panic of schoolboys caught smoking behind the bike sheds by the gym master.

Ian practically fell through his own rose bush, thorns snagging at his coat and one catching his wrist with a gentle, accusing scratch.

He didn't stop until he reached his back door. Fumbling the keys. The lock turned with a damp clack. He stepped inside and kicked the door closed behind him.

Soaked. Scratched. And suddenly very aware he'd spent nearly two hours in a hedge opposite a man with a Staffordshire ceramic dog named Gladys.

He peeled off his dripping jacket, mud flecked up his back, thorns still embedded in the cuff of his sleeve.

From the lounge, Susan's voice drifted out, calm and curious:

"Good bat-watching session, Daddy?"

Ian appeared around the corner; one eyebrow raised. "Very productive," he said solemnly, flicking a snail off his collar. "Full wingspan, firm sonar, mildly hostile."

Susan peered at him over the top of her magazine. "Please don't use the good tea towel to dry off this time."

He offered a vague grunt and disappeared into the kitchen, boots squelching softly on the slate tile floor.

*Time to escalate* Ian thought. He powered up his encrypted phone. Tapped out a quick message: *URGENT! TARGET DUFFY POSSIBLY COMPROMISED. REQUEST TEAM FOR INTERVENTION ASAP.*

He hit send.

Seconds later, the reply pinged back: *STAND BY. EXTRACTION PLANNED 0600 HOURS.*

Ian grinned, wolfed down a cold sausage roll, and collapsed onto the sofa with a warming class of 12-year-old Jameson's. Tomorrow was going to be interesting.

\*\*\*

Ian got up early before anyone – even Tolsoy – was awake.

The world was grey and wet as Ian gathered with three other agents in unmarked waterproofs.

Jim, his longtime MI5 contact, stood at the front, yawning into a polystyrene cup of tea.

"You look thrilled," Ian said.

"Got dragged out of bed at five bloody a.m. to bust a man who collects porcelain Labradors," Jim muttered.

"Don't underestimate the Staffordshire Mafia," Ian said, deadpan.

Jim snorted. "Right, let's knock."

The front door gave under Ian's shoulder with a reluctant creak, hinges complaining like an old man getting up from an all-too-soft armchair. The house beyond was silent. Not the stillness of sleep – not that warm domestic quiet of slippers unmanned and ticking clocks and Radio 4 drifting from the kitchen. No. This was the silence of vacancy. Of deliberate absence. Of someone who had vanished themselves.

The air was stale, tinged faintly with lavender furniture polish and that faint ozone trace of recently unplugged appliances. The kind of smell that said: No one's lived here for a while, and no one's coming back.

Ian stepped inside slowly, his boots brushing across the threshold with a low, hollow scrape.

The hallway, once lined with portraits of dogs and laminated charity calendars, was now bare. Hooks on the wall sat empty. The doormat was gone. Even the umbrella stand – that hideous twisted brass number shaped like a heron – had vanished.

He moved forward, each footstep louder than the last.

Kitchen – stripped. No kettle, no mugs, no fridge magnets. The spice rack had been unscrewed from the wall. Even the clock was missing. Only the faint outlines remained – ghosts of domesticity, squares of unfaded wallpaper that marked what had once been there.

Bedroom – empty. The bed frame gone. Curtains gone. Fitted wardrobe doors open, hangers swinging gently like abandoned gallows. Not a sock, not a receipt, not a single stray button.

Bathroom – gutted. Towel rail removed. Mirror gone. Only the silicone outline of where it had once clung. No shampoo. No toothbrush. Just a blank, sanitised void.

Ian's dread mounted with every step. He moved faster now, opening doors, scanning corners, kicking aside dust bunnies that shouldn't have existed in a house this previously meticulous.

No Duffy. No bear-man. No traces. Not even a teaspoon left behind.

And then – he entered the living room.

Again, completely bare. The bookshelves – gone. The floral sofa that had looked like it might suffocate you in doilies – vanished without a trace. Even the television stand had been taken. The socket where the aerial had plugged in still wept plaster dust. And there, in the centre of the bare mantelpiece, sat a single object. An abandoned ceramic spaniel. Just one, on its own. Small(ish). Earthenware. One of a classic Staffordshire pair. Except this one was broken – the left ear missing, a hairline crack running down the neck. Its eyes stared out with a weird, glazed vacancy, and its painted fur was dappled in blood-red glaze that now looked more like a warning than mere decoration.

Ian stepped forward slowly, the soles of his boots making soft hissing sounds on the dusty floor.

He reached out and picked it up. It was heavier than it should've been. Solid. Cold. The underside felt strange – slightly ridged, almost mechanical. He turned it over in his hands, frowning. Inside, instead of the usual hollow clink of cheap ceramic, there was the dull weight of something buried. He slipped it into a padded evidence pouch and sealed it with a smooth practiced flick of the wrist.

"We'll take it for DNA testing," he said, voice low, still scanning the room like the furniture might be hiding in the walls. "Maybe it'll tell us who he is and help work out where the bastard went."

Behind him, Jim stood in the doorway, trench coat damp from the drizzle, hands shoved deep into his pockets.

"Doubt it," he said flatly, squinting around at the surgically empty room. "Place is cleaner than a nun's browser history."

Ian exhaled through his nose, sharp and thin. He took one last slow turn through the room – seeing the pale outlines on the walls where pictures had once hung. The faint oval shape on the floor where an ottoman used to sit. A half-circle of slightly less-faded carpet by the door, where a chair leg must have pressed for years.

Gone. All of it. Clean. Professional. Timed to the hour.

No hasty getaway. No smashed drawers or trailing wires. Just a quiet, complete erasure.

Ian didn't like it.

He felt the first pang of it deep in his stomach – not fear. Not surprise.

Admiration.

That was worse.

He hated being played. Especially by men who wore sweater vests and collected ceramic dogs.

He looked at the evidence pouch again. And silently vowed to find out exactly who the hell had been sitting beneath all that honeysuckle and mildness.

Ian trudged back across the road.

Home.

Susan was watering the back garden, Tolstoy ambling behind her, sniffing things with deep suspicion.

Ian gave her a weary wave and slumped into the kitchen.

She asked, "Been for a walk Daddy?"

"Yes, had a bit of a headache. Didn't sleep very well last night," Ian replied

He made tea. Proper tea. No whisky – not yet.

He stared out the window, mind ticking.

Duffy had played a long game. A deep cover game. Just like Alison. And Ian had almost missed it. Almost.

The house had settled into its usual murmur – the low hum of the boiler, the occasional creak of floorboards adjusting to the drop in temperature, and the distant, familiar rattle of Susan loading the dishwasher with theatrical sighs.

Ian sat slouched on the sagging living room sofa like a man who had both nothing and everything on his mind. A mug of builder's tea – 60% Glenfiddich by volume – now sat half-drunk on the side table, the rim stained with bacon grease from the sandwich he'd forgotten he'd just eaten.

His socks were mismatched. His jumper had a baked bean fossilised near the hem.

Tolstoy, stretched out across the hearthrug, snored like a diesel generator under a duvet.

The telly was on but muted. Some documentary about beavers building a dam. Captivating in its own right, but Ian wasn't watching. His eyes were closed. One hand tucked into his waistband like an old man napping through a Sunday sermon.

Then the phone buzzed. That phone. The black one – wedge-shaped, unbranded, no ringtones, no notifications, no way to trace it unless you were already in too deep to care. Ian's eyes opened.

He snatched it up from where it buzzed against the cracked leather armrest.

One new message. Just a few words.

*DNA MATCH FROM BROKEN DOG. CONFIRMED IDENTITY: FORMER KGB WET WORK OPERATOR. LINKED TO PRAGUE ASSASSINATION, 2016. HIGH-LEVEL CLEARANCE..*

*DOG CONTAINED C5 EXPLOSIVE CHARGE – BOOBY TRAPPED BUT FAILED TO GO OFF! LUCKY!*

Ian stared at the screen. Then gave a low, tuneless whistle through his teeth.

Prague, 2016.

That had been a bad one. An arms broker gassed in his hotel bathroom. Nerve agent hidden in a bar of hotel soap. Two bellboys hospitalised. A maid blinded. No witnesses, no footprints. Just one blurry CCTV still of a large man, with a bald head in a flat cap. It had gone unsolved.

Until now.

Ian leaned forward, elbows on his knees, and scrolled through the gallery on his secure phone. The photos he'd taken during his surveillance of Duffy.

Malcolm Duffy. In his hedge. Out with the bins. Watering his hydrangeas with psychotic diligence. And the bear-man. Only one clear photo – taken through the misted lens of the night-vision binoculars – but the shape was there. The size. The posture. A neck thick enough to require planning permission.

Ian had faces. Movements. Routine. Heights. Gait. Preferred coats. Enough to hunt them. Not today. Maybe not even this year. But eventually.

They'd slipped through the net this time – vanished like ghosts into the drizzle of the early morning.

But he had their scent now. And Ian, like Tolstoy, didn't forget scents.

He leaned back into the cushions, the sofa groaning beneath him. Crumbs cascaded from his jumper like sad confetti. Tolstoy shifted, let out a deep, expressive fart, and resettled with a sigh.

Outside, the rain intensified – rhythmic, relentless, like a war drum in the dark. Ian tilted his head, watching the drops streak down the glass like tears. He scratched his chest absently and muttered to no one: "Always the quiet ones."

Susan called from the kitchen. "Do you want toast or not, Daddy?"

He glanced toward the kitchen door. "Nah. I'm full of rage and vengeance, thanks."

She didn't reply.

The lights dimmed slightly, then settled. Somewhere, a radiator hissed.

Ian smiled faintly. He reached for the mug, took a long sip, and let the whisky scald his throat.

This wasn't over. Not even close. There were men to find. Questions to answer. Ceramic dogs to impound. Loose ends that weren't as loose as they looked.

He reached for the TV remote and unmuted the documentary that was playing.

On screen, the beavers were still at it. Building. Burrowing. Waiting out the storm.

*Smart bastards,* Ian thought.

The camera panned over the dam – sturdy, quiet, perfectly disguised.

He narrowed his eyes slightly.

There was always something going on under the surface. Always.

Printed in Dunstable, United Kingdom